# HAUNTED IN DEA...
# AND ETERNITY IN DEATH

Plɛ

enant Eve Dallas doesn't believe in ghosts. But *aunted in Death*, when a very recent corpse s s up in an abandoned nightclub, alongside the b s of famous missing singer Bobbie Bray, e yone is spooked. Did Bobbie's ghost finally get her revenge, or is there a more earthly explanation? W e in *Eternity in Death*, when notorious It-girl Tiara Kent is found dead in her plush Manhattan apartment, the murder looks to everyone like a vampire attack — everyone but the practical Lieutenant Eve Dallas. Discovering Tiara's secret lover, Eve and her team are led on a chase into the darkest corners of the city and deep into their own

# SPECIAL MESSAGE TO READERS

## THE ULVERSCROFT FOUNDATION
**(registered UK charity number 264873)**
was established in 1972 to provide funds for
research, diagnosis and treatment of eye diseases.
Examples of major projects funded by
the Ulverscroft Foundation are:-

- The Children's Eye Unit at Moorfields Eye Hospital, London
- The Ulverscroft Children's Eye Unit at Great Ormond Street Hospital for Sick Children
- Funding research into eye diseases and treatment at the Department of Ophthalmology, University of Leicester
- The Ulverscroft Vision Research Group, Institute of Child Health
- Twin operating theatres at the Western Ophthalmic Hospital, London
- The Chair of Ophthalmology at the Royal Australian College of Ophthalmologists

You can help further the work of the Foundation
by making a donation or leaving a legacy.
Every contribution is gratefully received. If you
would like to help support the Foundation or
require further information, please contact:

**THE ULVERSCROFT FOUNDATION**
**The Green, Bradgate Road, Anstey**
**Leicester LE7 7FU, England**
**Tel: (0116) 236 4325**

**website: www.foundation.ulverscroft.com**

# HAUNTED IN DEATH
# AND
# ETERNITY IN DEATH

## J. D. ROBB

ISIS
LARGE
PRINT

First published in Great Britain 2013
by
Piatkus
an imprint of
Little, Brown Book Group

First Isis Edition
published 2015
by arrangement with
Little, Brown Book Group
An Hachette UK Company

A catalogue record for this book is available
from the British Library.

ISBN 978–1–78541–088–8 (hb)
ISBN 978–1–78541–094–9 (pb)

Published by
F. A. Thorpe (Publishing)
Anstey, Leicestershire

Set by Words & Graphics Ltd.
Anstey, Leicestershire
Printed and bound in Great Britain by
T. J. International Ltd., Padstow, Cornwall

This book is printed on acid-free paper

# HAUNTED
# IN DEATH

There nearly always is method in madness.

G.K. CHESTERTON


There needs no ghost, my lord, come from the grave to tell us this.

WILLIAM SHAKESPEARE

# CHAPTER
# ONE

Winter could be murderous. The slick streets and icy sidewalks broke bones and cracked skulls with gleeful regularity. Plummeting temperatures froze the blood and stopped the hearts of a select few every night in the frigid misery of Sidewalk City.

Even those lucky enough to have warm, cozy homes were trapped inside by the bitter winds and icy rains. In the first two weeks of January 2060 — post-holiday — bitch winter was a contributing factor to the sharp rise in domestic disturbance calls to the New York City Police and Security Department.

Even reasonably happy couples got twitchy when they were bound together long enough by the cold ropes of winter.

For Lieutenant Eve Dallas, double d's weren't on her plate. Unless some stir-crazy couple killed each other out of sheer boredom.

She was Homicide.

On this miserable, bone-chilling morning, she stood over the dead. It wasn't the cold or the ice that had killed Radcliff C. Hopkins III. She couldn't say, as yet, if the blue-tipped fingers of winter had been a contributing factor. But it was clear someone had put numerous nasty holes in Radcliff C.'s chest. And another, neatly centered on his wide forehead.

Beside her, Eve's partner Detective Delia Peabody crouched for a closer look. "I've never seen these kinds of wounds before, outside of training vids."

"I have. Once."

It had been winter then, too, Eve remembered, when she'd stood over the first victim in a series of rape/murders. The gun ban had all but eliminated death by firearm, so gunshot wounds were rare. Not that people didn't continue to kill each other habitually. But the remote violence and simplicity of a bullet into flesh and bone wasn't often the method of choice these days.

Radcliff C. might have been done in by an antiquated method, but it didn't make him any less dead.

"Lab boys will rub their hands together over this one," Eve murmured. "They don't get much call to play with ballistics."

She was a tall woman, with a lean build inside a long black leather coat. Her face was sharp with angles, her eyes long and brown and observant. As a rare concession to the cold, she'd yanked a black watch cap over her short, usually untidy brown hair. But she'd lost her gloves again.

She continued to stand, let her partner run the gauge for time of death.

"Six wounds visible," Eve said. "Four in the body, one in the right leg, one to the head. From the blood spatter, blood trail, it looks like he was hit first there."

She gestured a few feet away. "Force knocks him back, down, so he tries to crawl. Big guy, fleshy, with a strong look to him. He maybe had enough in him to crawl some, maybe to try to get up again."

"Time of death, oh-two-twenty." Peabody, her dark hair in a short, sassy flip at the base of her neck, looked up. Her square, sturdy face was cop solemn, but there was a gleam in her eye, dark as her hair. "ID confirmed. You know who he is, right?"

"Hopkins, Radcliff C. With the fussy Roman numerals after."

"Your lack of interest in culture trivia's showing again. His grandfather was Hop Hopkins, and he made a couple of fortunes in the swinging Sixties. Nineteen-sixties. Sex, drugs and rock 'n' roll. Night clubs, music venues. LA-based, mostly, before the big one hit California, but he had a hot spot here in New York."

Peabody shifted her weight. "Ran hot for a couple of decades, then hit a serious patch of bad luck. The even more legendary Bobbie Bray — she was —"

"I know who Bobbie Bray was." Eve hooked her thumbs in her pockets, rocking back on her heels as she continued to study the body, the scene. "I'm not completely oblivious to popular culture. Rock star, junkie, and a cult figure now. Vanished without a trace."

"Yeah, well, she was his wife — third or fourth — when she poofed. Rumor and gossip figured maybe he offed her or had her done, but the cops couldn't find enough evidence to indict. He went spooky, did the hermit thing, lost big fat piles of dough, and ended up

7

OD'ing on his drug of choice — can't remember what it was — right here in New York."

Peabody pushed to her feet. "From there it's urban legend time. Place where he OD'd was upstairs from the club, that's where he'd holed himself up. In the luxury apartment he'd put in on the top floor. Building passed from hand to hand, but nobody could ever make a go of it. Because . . ."

Peabody paused now, for effect. "It's haunted. And cursed. Anyone who's ever tried to live there, or put a business in, suffers personal and/or physical misfortunes."

"Number Twelve. Yeah, I've heard of it. Interesting." Hands still in her pockets, Eve scanned the large, dilapidated room. "Haunted and cursed. Seems redundant. Guess maybe Radcliff C. figured on bucking that."

"What do you mean?" Then Peabody's jaw dropped. "This is the place? *This?* Oh boy. Jeez."

"Anonymous tip does the nine-one-one. Gonna want to review that transmission, because it's likely it was the killer. What I've got is the vic owned the building, was having it rehabbed, redesigned. Maybe looking for some of his grandfather's glory days. But what's our boy doing hanging around in a cursed, haunted building at two in the morning?"

"This is the place," Peabody repeated, reverently now. "Number Twelve."

"Since the addy's Twelve East Twelfth, I'm going to go out on a limb and say, yeah. Let's turn him."

"Oh, right."

When they rolled the body, Eve pursed her lips. "Somebody really wanted this guy dead. Three more entry wounds on the back. Lab will confirm, but I'm thinking . . ."

She crossed the room toward a set of old circular iron stairs. "Standing about here, facing the attacker. Pow, pow. Takes it in the chest." She slapped a hand on her own. "Stumbles back, goes down. The smeared blood trail tells me the vic tried crawling away, probably toward the doors."

"Doors were locked from the inside. First on scene said," Peabody added.

"Yeah. So he's crawling, and the killer moves in. Pow, pow, into the back." *The sound of the shots must have blasted the air in here*, Eve thought. *Must have set the ears ringing.* "But it's not enough. No, we're not finished yet. Body falls, has to be dead or dying, but it's not enough. Turns the body over, puts the barrel of the gun to the forehead. See the burn marks around the forehead wound? Contact. I did a lot of studying up on firearms during the DeBlass case a couple years ago. Puts the barrel right against the head and pow. Coup de grace."

Eve saw it in her head. Heard it, smelled it. "You put a gun like this." She pressed her fingertip to her own brow. "You put it right against the skin and fire, it's personal. You put that many steel missiles in somebody, you're seriously pissed off."

"Vic's got his bright, shiny wristwatch — looks antique — his wallet — cash and credit inside — key codes, PPC, pocket 'link. Killer didn't bother making it look like robbery."

"We'll run the electronics. Let's have a look at the 'link."

Eve took the 'link in her sealed hands, called up the last transmission. There was a whispering, windy sound which Eve had to admit tingled her spine just a bit. The husky female voice wove through it.

*Number Twelve. Two* A.M. *Bring it. Bring it, and we'll party.*

"Maybe robbery plays in after all."

"Did you hear that voice?" Peabody sent a cautious look over her shoulder. "It sounded, you know, unearthly."

"Funny, sounded computer-generated to me. But maybe that's because I know ghosts don't make 'link transmissions, or shoot guns. Because — and this may be news to you, Peabody — ghosts don't exist."

Peabody only shook her head, sagely. "Oh yeah? Tell that to my great-aunt Josie who died eight years ago and came back half a dozen times to nag my great-uncle Phil about fixing the leaky toilet in the powder room. She left him alone after he called the plumber."

"And how much does your great-uncle Phil drink?"

"Oh, come on. People see ghosts all the time."

"That's because people, by and large, are whacked. Let's work the case, Peabody. It wasn't a ghostly finger that pulled the trigger here. Or lured the vic to an empty building in the middle of the night. Let's do a

**10**

run. Spouse, family, beneficiaries, business partners, friends, enemies. And let's keep it to the corporeal."

Eve re-examined the body, wondering if he'd brought whatever *it* was. "They can bag and tag. Start checking doors and windows. Let's find out how the killer got out of the building. I'll have another talk with the first on scene."

"You want me to stay in here? To wander around in here. Alone?"

"Are you kidding?" One look at Peabody's face told Eve her partner was absolutely serious. "Well, for God's sake. You take the first on scene. I'll take the building."

"Better plan. You want crime scene in now, and the body transported?"

"Get it done."

Eve took a visual sweep on the main floor. Maybe it had been a hot spot in the last century, but now it was derelict. She could see where some of the work had begun. Portions of the grimy walls had been stripped away to their bones to reveal the old, and certainly out-of-code, electrical wiring. Portable lights and heating units were set up, as well as stacks of materials in what seemed to be tidy and organized piles.

But the drop cloths, the material, the lights all had a coat of dust. Maybe Hopkins had started his rehab, but it looked as if there'd been a long lag since the last nail gun popped.

The remains of an old bar hulked in the center of the room. As it was draped with more dusty protective cloth, she assumed Hopkins had intended to restore it to whatever its former glory might have been.

11

She checked the rear exit door, found it too secured from inside. Through another door she found what might have been a storeroom at one time, and was now a junk heap. The two windows were about big enough for a cat to squeeze through, and were riot barred.

The toilet facilities on the main level were currently pits, with no outside access.

"Okay, unless you're still here, waiting for me to cuff you and read you your rights, you found a way up and out."

She glanced at the ancient elevator; opted for the spindly iron stairs.

The sweepers were going to have a hell of a time finding usable prints or physical evidence, she thought. There were decades of dust, grime, considerable water damage, what seemed to be old scorching from a fire.

She recorded and marked some blurry footprints smudged on the dirty floor.

*Cold*, she thought. *Freaking cold in here.*

She moved along the second floor landing, imagined it packed with tables and people during its heyday. Music pumping out to shatter eardrums, the fashionable drugs of the time passed around like party favors. The chrome safety railings would have been polished to a gleam, flashing with the wild colors of the lights.

She stood as she was a moment, looking down as the ME drones bagged the body. Good view from there, she mused. See whatever you want to see. People ass to elbow below, sweating and grinding on the dance floor and hoping somebody was watching.

*Did you come up here tonight, Hopkins? Did you have enough brains before they got blown out to come early, scope the place out? Or did you just walk in?*

She found the exit at a second story window, unlocked and partially open, with the emergency stairs deployed.

"So much for that mystery. Suspect most likely exited the building," she stated for the record, "from this point. Sweepers will process the window, stairs and surrounding areas for prints and other evidence. And lookie, lookie." She crouched, shined her light on the edge of the windowsill. "Got a little blood, probably vic's. Suspect may have had some spatter, or transferred some blood to his clothing when he moved in for the head shot."

Frowning, she shined the light further down, onto the floor where something sparkled. "Looks like jewelry. Or . . . hmm. Some sort of hair decoration," she amended when she lifted it with tweezers. "Damn if it doesn't look like diamonds to me, on some kind of clip. About a half inch wide, maybe two inches long. No dust on it — stones are clean and bright in what I'd guess to be a platinum setting. Antique-looking."

She bagged it.

She started to head back down, then thought she heard the floor creak overhead. Old buildings, she reminded herself, but drew her weapon. She moved to the back wall, which was partially caved in, and the old metal stairs behind it.

The sound came again, just a stealthy little creak. For a moment she thought she heard a woman's voice, raw and throaty, singing about a bleeding heart.

At the top of the stairs the floors had been scrubbed clean. They were scarred and scorched, but no dust lay on them. There was old smoke and fire damage on some of the interior walls, but she could see the area had been set up into a large apartment, and what might have been an office.

She swept, light and weapon, but saw nothing but rubble. The only sound now was the steady inhale, exhale of her own breath, which came out in veritable plumes.

If heat was supposed to rise, why the hell was it so much colder up here? She moved through the doorless opening to the left to do a thorough search.

Floors are too clean, she thought. And there was no debris here as there was in the other smaller unit, no faded graffiti decorating the walls. Eve cocked her head at the large hole in the wall on the far right. It looked as though it had been measured and cut, neatly, as a doorway.

She crossed the room to shine her light into the dark.

The skeleton lay as if in repose. In the center of the skull's forehead was a small, almost tidy hole.

Cupped in the yellowed fingers was the glittery mate to the diamond clip. And near the other was the chrome gleam of a semi-automatic.

"Well son of a bitch," Eve murmured, and pulled out her communicator to hail Peabody.

# CHAPTER
# TWO

"It's her. It's got to be her."

"Her being the current vic's ancestor's dead wife." Eve drove through spitting ice from the crime scene to the victim's home.

"Or lover. I'm not sure they were actually married now that I think about it. Gonna check on that," Peabody added, making a note in her memo book. "But here's what must've gone down: Hopkins, the first one, kills Bobbie, then bricks the body up in the wall of the apartment he used over the club."

"And the cops at the time didn't notice there was a spanking new brick wall in the apartment?"

"Maybe they didn't look very hard. Hopkins had a lot of money, and a river of illegal substances. A lot of connections, and probably a lot of information certain high connections wouldn't want made public."

"He bought off the investigation." Whether it happened eighty-five years ago or yesterday, the smell of bad cops offended Eve's senses. But ... "Not impossible," she had to admit. "If it is the missing wife/girlfriend, it could be she wasn't reported missing until he had everything fairly tidied up. Then you got your payoff, or classic blackmail regarding the investigators, and he walks clean."

"He did sort of go crazy. Jeez, Dallas, he basically locked himself up there in that place for over ten years, with a body behind the wall."

"Maybe. Let's get the bones dated and identified before we jump there. The crime scene guys were all but weeping with joy over those bones. While they're having their fun, we've got an active case, from this century."

"But you're curious, right? You gotta wonder if we just found Bobbie Bray. And the hair clips. Is that spooky or what?"

"Nothing spooky about a killer planting them. Wanted us to find the bones, that's a given. So connecting the dots, the skeleton and our vic are linked, at least in the killer's mind. What do we have on Hopkins so far?"

"Vic was sixty-two at TOD. Three marriages, three divorces. Only offspring — son from second marriage." Peabody scanned her memo book. "Bounced back and forth between New York and New LA, with a couple of stints in Europe. Entertainment field, mostly fringe. Didn't seem to have his grandfather's flair. Parents died in a private plane crash twenty-five years back. No sibs."

Peabody glanced over. "The Hopkins line doesn't go toward longevity and propagation. Part of the curse."

"Part of birth control practices and lousy luck," Eve corrected. "What else — salient — do we have?"

"You gotta wonder," Peabody went on. "I mean Hopkins number two was married four times. Four. One surviving son — or surviving until now. He had a daughter from another marriage who drowned when she was a teenager, and another son — still another marriage — who hanged himself when he was twenty-three. That's the kind of consistent bad luck that says curse to me."

"It says pretty irrelevant background data to me. Give me something on our vic."

"Okay, okay. Rad Hopkins went through a lot of the money his father managed to recoup, and most of what he'd inherited from his mother, who was a socialite with some traces of blue blood. He had a few minor smudges for illegals, solicitation, gray-area business practices. No time served. Oh, no collector's license for firearms."

"Where are the ex-wives?"

"Number one's based in New LA, B-movie actress. Well, B-minus, really. Number three's in Europe, married to some minor English aristocrat. But Number two's here in New York. Fanny Gill — dance instructor. The son's Cliff Gill Hopkins — though he dropped the Hopkins legally at age twenty-one. They run a dance studio."

"New York's an easy place to get to and get out of. We'll run them all. Business partners?"

"None currently. He's had a mess of them, off and on. But he was the sole owner and proprietor of Number Twelve Productions, which has the same address as his residence. He bought the building he died in at auction about six months ago."

"Not much work done in there in six months."

"I tagged the construction company from the name on the building permit. Owner tells me they got called off after three weeks. Their scuttlebutt is Hopkins ran out of money, and scrambled around for some backers. But he said he had a call from the vic a few days ago, wanting to schedule work to start up again."

"So maybe he got some money, or wheeled some sort of deal."

She found the miracle of a street-level spot a half block from Hopkins's building.

"Decent digs," Eve noted. "Fancy antique wrist unit, designer wallet, pricey shoes. Doesn't give the appearance of hurting financially."

She flashed her badge at the doorman. "Hopkins," she said. "Radcliff C."

"I'll ring up and let him know you'd like to speak with him."

"Don't bother. He's in the morgue. When's the last time you saw him?"

"Dead?" The doorman, a short, stocky mixed-race man of about forty, stared at Eve as his jaw dropped. "Mr Hopkins is dead? An accident?"

"Yes, he's dead. No, it wasn't an accident. When did you last see him?"

"Yesterday. He went out about twelve-thirty in the afternoon, came back around two. I went off duty at four. My replacement would have gone off at midnight. No doorman from midnight to eight."

"Anybody come to see him?"

"No one that checked in with me. The building's secured. Passcodes are required for the elevators. Mr Hopkins's apartment is on the sixth floor." The doorman shook his head, rubbed a gloved hand over the back of his neck. "Dead. I just can't believe it."

"He live alone?"

"He did, yes."

"Entertain much?"

"Occasionally."

"Overnight entertaining? Come on, Cleeve," Eve prompted, scanning his brass name tag. "Guy's dead."

"Occasionally," he repeated and puffed out his cheeks. "He, ah, liked variety, so I couldn't say there was any particular lady. He also liked them young."

"How young?"

"Mid-twenties, primarily, by my gauge. I haven't noticed anyone visiting the last couple of weeks. He's been in and out nearly every day. Meetings, I assume, for the club he's opening. Was opening."

"Okay, good enough. We're going up."

"I'll clear the code for you." Cleeve held the door for them, then walked to the first of two elevators. He skimmed his passcode through the slot, then keyed in his code. "I'm sorry to hear about Mr Hopkins," he said as the doors opened. "He never gave me any trouble."

"Not a bad epitaph," Eve decided as the elevator headed up to six.

The apartment was single-level, but spacious. Particularly since it was nearly empty of furnishings. There was a sleep chair in the living room, facing a wall screen. There were a multitude of high-end electronics and carton after carton of entertainment discs. It was all open space with a colored-glass wall separating the sleeping area.

"There was art on the walls," Eve noted. "You can see the squares and rectangles of darker paint where they must've hung. Probably sold them to get some capital for his project."

A second bedroom was set up as an office, and from the state of it, Eve didn't judge Hopkins had been a tidy or organized businessman. The desk was heaped with scribbled notes, sketches, memo cubes, coffee cups and plates from working meals.

A playback of the desk 'link was loaded with oily conversation with the recently deceased pitching his project to potential backers or arranging meetings where she supposed he'd have been doing the same.

"Let's have EDD go through all the data and communication." The Electronic Detective Division could comb through the transmissions and data faster and more efficiently than she. "Doesn't look like he's entertained here recently, which jibes with our doorman's statement. Nothing personal in the last little while on his home 'link. It's all about money."

She walked through the apartment. The guy wasn't living there so much as surviving. Selling off his stuff, scrambling for capital. "The motive's not all about money, though. He couldn't have had enough for that. The motive's emotional. It's personal. Kill him where the yellowing bones of a previous victim are hidden. Purposeful. Building was auctioned off six months ago? Private or public?"

"I can check," Peabody began.

"I got a quicker source."

It seemed to her the guy she'd married was always in, on his way to or coming back from some meeting. Then again, he seemed to like them. It took all kinds.

And she had to admit when that face of his filled her screen, it put a little boost in her step to think: *mine*.

"Quick question," she began. "Number Twelve. Any details on its auction?"

His dark brows raised over those intense blue eyes. "Bought for a song, which will likely turn out to be a dirge. Or has it already?" Roarke asked her.

"You're quick, too. Yeah, current owner's in the morgue. He got it on the cheap?"

"Previous owners had it on the market for several years, and put it up for public auction a few months ago after the last fire."

"Fire?"

"There've been several. Unexplained," he added with that Irish lilt cruising through his voice. "Hopkins, wasn't it? Descendent of infamy. How was he killed?"

"Nine millimeter Smith and Wesson."

Surprise moved over that extraordinary face. "Well now. Isn't that interesting? You recovered the weapon, I take it."

"Yeah, I got it. Fill you in on that later. The auction, you knew about it, right?"

"I did. It was well-publicized for several weeks. A building with that history generates considerable media attention as well."

"Yeah, that's what I figured. If it was a bargain, why didn't you snap it up to add it to your mega-Monopoly board?"

"Haunted. Cursed."

"Yeah, right." She snorted out a laugh, but he only continued to look out from the screen. "Okay, thanks. See you later."

"You certainly will."

"Couldn't you just listen to him?" Peabody let out a sigh. "I mean couldn't you just close your eyes and listen?"

"Snap out of it, Peabody. Hopkins's killer had to know the building was up for sale. Maybe he bid on it, maybe he didn't. He doesn't move on the previous owners, but waits for Hopkins. Goes back to personal. Lures him, kills him, leaves the weapon and the hair clips with the skeleton behind the brick. Making a statement."

Peabody huffed out a breath. "This place doesn't make much of a statement, personal or otherwise."

"Let's toss it anyway. Then we're going dancing."

The Gill School of Dance was on the third floor of a stubby post-Urban War building on the West Side. It boasted a large, echoing room with a mirrored wall, a barre, a huddle of chairs and a decorative screen that sectioned off a minute desk.

The space smelled of sweat heavily covered with floral air freshener.

Fanny Gill herself was skinny as an eel, with a hard, suspicious face and a lot of bright blond hair tied up with a red scarf. Her pinched face went even tighter as she set her tiny ass on the desk.

"So somebody killed the rat bastard. When's the funeral? I got a red dress I've been saving for a special occasion."

"No love lost, Ms Gill?"

"Oh, all of it lost, honey. My boy out there?" She jerked a chin toward the screen. On the other side, a man in a sleeveless skinsuit was calling out time and steps to a group of grubby-looking ballerinas. "He's the only decent thing I ever got from Rad the Bad. I was twenty-two years old, fresh and green as a head of iceberg."

She didn't sigh so much as snort, as if to signal those salad days were long over.

"I sure did fall for him. He had a line, that bastard, he had a way. Got married, got pregnant. Had a little money, about twenty thou? He took it, *invested* it." Her lips flattened into one thin, red line. "Blew it, every dollar. Always going to wheel the deal, strike the big time. Like hell. Cheated on me, too. But I stuck, nearly ten years, because I wanted my boy to have a father. Finally figured out no father's better than a lousy one. Divorced him — hired a fucking shark lawyer — excuse the language."

"No problem. Cops hear words like *lawyer* all the time."

Fanny barked out a laugh, then seemed to relax. "Wasn't much to get, but I got my share. Enough to start this place up. And you know, that son of a bitch tried to hit me up for a loan? Called it a business

23

investment, of course. Just a couple months ago. Never changes."

"Was this business investment regarding Number Twelve?"

"Yeah, that's it. Like I'd have anything to do with that place — or Rad."

"Could you tell us where you were last night, Ms Gill? From say midnight to three?"

"In bed, asleep. I teach my first class at seven in the morning." She sniffed, looking more amused than offended to be considered a suspect in a homicide. "Hey, if I'd wanted to kill Rad, I'd've done it twenty years ago. You're going to ask my boy, too, aren't you?"

"It's routine."

Fanny nodded. "I sleep alone, but he doesn't."

"Dead? Murdered?" Cliff lowered the towel he'd used to dry his damp face. "How? When?"

"Early this morning. The how is classified for the moment. Can you give us your whereabouts between midnight and three?"

"We got home about one. We'd been out with friends. Um . . . give me a second." He picked up a bottle of water, stared at it, then drank. He was a well-built thirty, with streaked blond hair curling in a tail worn halfway down his back. "Lars Gavin, my cohab. We met some friends at Achilles. A club uptown. We went to bed right after we got home, and I got up about seven, seven-thirty. Sorry, I think I want to sit down."

"We're going to need names and contact information on the people you were with, and a number where we can reach your cohab."

"Yeah, sure. Okay. How? How did it happen?" He lifted dazed eyes to Eve's. "Was he mugged?"

"No. I'm not able to give you many details at this time. When's the last time you had contact with your father?"

"A couple months ago. He came by to try to hit my mother up for some money. Like that would work." Cliff managed a half smile, but it wobbled. "Then he put the line on me. I gave him five hundred."

He glanced over to where Fanny was running another group through barre exercises. "Mom'll skin me if she finds out, but I gave him the five."

"That's not the first time you gave him money," Eve deduced.

"No. I'd give him a few hundred now and then. It kept him off my mother's back, and we do okay here. The school, I mean. We do okay. And Lars, he understands."

"But this time he went to your mother first."

"Got to her before I could steer him off. Upsets her, you know? He figured he could sweet talk her out of a good chunk for this investment. Get rich deal — always a deal." Now Cliff scrubbed his hands over his face.

"They fight about it?" Eve asked him.

"No. My mother's done fighting with him. Been done a long time ago. And my father, he doesn't argue. He . . . he cajoles. Basically, she told him to come by again when Hell froze over. So he settled for me, on the sly, and the five hundred. He said he'd be in touch when the ball got rolling, but that was just another line. Didn't matter. It was only five. I don't know how to feel. I don't know how I'm supposed to feel."

"I can't tell you, Mr Gill. Why did you remove Hopkins from your legal name?"

"This place — Gill School of Dance. My mother." He lifted his shoulder, looked a little abashed. "And well, it's got a rep. Hopkins. It's just bad luck."

# CHAPTER
# THREE

Eve wasn't surprised MD Morris had snagged Hopkins. Multiple gunshot wounds had to be a happy song and dance for a medical examiner. An interesting change of pace from the stabbings, the bludgeonings, strangulations and overdoses.

Morris, resplendent in a bronze-toned suit under his clear protective cape, his long dark hair in a shining tail, stood over the body with a sunny smile for Eve.

"You send me the most interesting things."

"We do what we can," Eve said. "What can you tell me I don't already know?"

"Members of one family of the fruit fly are called peacocks because they strut on the fruit."

"Huh. I'll file that one. Let's be more specific. What can you tell me about our dead guy?"

"The first four wounds — chest — and the leg wound — fifth — could have been repaired with timely medical intervention. The next severed the spine, the seventh damaged the kidney. Number eight was a slight wound, meaty part of the shoulder. But he was dead by then. The final, close contact, entered the brain, which had already closed down shop."

He gestured to his wall screen, and called up a program. "The first bullets entered at a near level angle." Morris continued as the graphics played out on-screen. "You see, the computer suggested, and I concur, that the assailant fired four times, rapidly, hitting body mass. The victim fell after the fourth shot."

Eve studied the reenactment as Morris did, noting the graphic of the victim took the first two shots standing, the second two slightly hunched forward in the beginning of a fall.

"Big guy," Peabody commented. "Stumbles back a little, but keeps his feet for the first couple shots. I've only seen training and entertainment vids with gun death," she added. "I'd have thought the first shot would slap him down."

"His size, the shock of the impact," Morris said, "and the rapidity of fire would have contributed to the delay in his fall. Again, from the angles by which the bullets entered the body, it's likely he stumbled back, then lurched forward slightly, then went down — knee, heels of the hand taking the brunt of the fall."

He turned to Eve. "Your report indicated that the blood pattern showed the victim tried to crawl or pull himself away across the floor."

"That'd be right."

"As he did, the assailant followed, firing over and down, according to the angle of the wounds in the back, leg, shoulder."

Eyes narrowed now, Eve studied the computer-generated replay. "Stalking him, firing while he's down. Bleeding, crawling. You ever shoot a gun, Morris?"

"Actually, no."

"I have," she continued. "Feels interesting in your hand. Gives this little kick when it fires. Makes you part of it, that little jolt. Runs through you. I'm betting the killer was juiced on that. The jolt, the *bang*! Gotta be juiced to put more missiles into a guy who's crawling away, leaving his blood smeared on the floor."

"People always find creative and ugly ways to kill. I'd have said using a gun makes the kill less personal. But it doesn't feel that way in this case."

She nodded. "Yeah, this was personal, almost intimate. The ninth shot in particular."

"For the head shot, the victim — who as you say had considerable girth — had to be shoved or rolled over. At that time, the gun was pressed to the forehead. There's not only burning and residue, but a circular bruising pattern. When I'm able to compare it, I'm betting my share that it matches the dimensions of the gun barrel. The killer pressed the gun down into the forehead before he fired."

"See how you like *that*, you bastard," Eve murmured.

"Yes, indeed. Other than being riddled with bullets, your vic was in reasonably good health, despite being about twenty pounds overweight. He dyed his hair, had an eye and chin tuck within the last five years. He'd last eaten about two hours prior to death. Soy chips, sour pickles, processed cheese, washed down with domestic beer."

"The bullets?"

"On their way to the lab. I ran them through my system first. Nine millimeter." Morris switched programs so that images of the spent bullets he'd recovered came on screen.

"Man, it messes them up, doesn't it?"

"It doesn't do tidy work on flesh, bone and organ either. The vic had no gunpowder residue on his hands, no defensive wounds. Bruising on the left knee, which would have been inflicted when he fell. As well as some scraping on the heels of both hands, consistent with the fall on the floor surface."

"So he didn't fight back, or have the chance to. Didn't turn away." She angled her own body as if preparing for flight. "No indication he tried to run when and if he saw the gun."

"That's not what his body tells me."

Nor was it what it had told her on scene.

"A guy doesn't usually snack on chips and pickles if he's nervous or worried," Peabody put in. "Run of his entertainment unit showed he last viewed a soft porn vid about the time he'd have had the nibbles. This meet didn't have him sweating."

"Somebody he knew and figured he could handle," Eve agreed. She looked at the body again. "Guess he was dead wrong about that one."

"Number Twelve," Morris said as Eve turned to go.

"That's right."

"So the legend of Bobbie Bray comes to a close."

"That would be the missing woman, presumed dead."

30

"It would. Gorgeous creature, Bobbie, with the voice of a tormented angel."

"If you remember Bobbie Bray, you're looking damn good for your age, Morris."

He flashed that smile again. "There are thousands of websites devoted to her, and a substantial cult following. Beautiful woman with her star just starting to rise vanishes. Poof! Of course, sightings of her continued for decades after. And talk of her ghost haunting Number Twelve continues even today. Cold spots, apparitions, music coming from thin air. You get any of that?"

Eve thought of the snatch of song, the deep chill. "What I've got, potentially, are her bones. They're real enough."

"I'll be working on them with the forensic anthropologist at the lab." Morris's smile stayed sunny. "Can't wait to get my hands on her."

Back at Central, Eve sat in her office to reconstruct Hopkins's last day. She'd verified his lunch meeting with a couple of local movers and shakers who were both alibied tight for the time in question. A deeper check of his financials showed a sporadic income over the past year from a shop called Bygones, with the last deposit mid-December.

"Still skimming it close, Rad. How the hell were you going to pay for the rehab? Expecting a windfall, maybe? What were you supposed to bring to Number Twelve last night?"

*Gets the call on his pocket 'link,* she mused. *Deliberately spooky. But he doesn't panic. Sits around, has a snack, watches some light porn.*

She sat back at her desk, closed her eyes. The security disc from Hopkins's building showed him leaving at 1:35. Alone. Looked like he was whistling a tune, Eve recalled. Not a care in the world. Not carrying anything. No briefcase, no package, no bag.

"Yo."

Eve opened her eyes and looked at Feeney. The EDD captain was comfortably rumpled, his wiry ginger hair exploding around his hangdog face. "Whatcha got?"

"More what you've got," he said and stepped into the office. "Number Twelve."

"Jeez, why does everybody keep saying that? Like it was its own country."

"Practically is. Hop Hopkins, Bobbie Bray, Andy Warhol, Mick Jagger." For a moment, Feeney looked like a devotee at a sacred altar. "Christ, Dallas, what a place it must've been when it was still rocking."

"It's a dump now."

"Cursed," he said, so casually she blinked.

"Get out. You serious?"

"As a steak dinner. Found bricked-up bones, didn't you? And a body, antique gun, diamonds. Stuff legends are made of. And it gets better."

"Oh yeah?"

He held up a disc. "Ran your vic's last incoming transmission and the nine-one-one, and for the hell of it, did a voice-print on both. Same voice on both. Guess whose it is?"

32

"Bobbie Bray's."

"Hey." He actually pouted.

"Has to figure. The killer did the computer-generated deal, used Bray's voice, probably pieced together from old media interviews and such. Unless you're going to sit there and tell me you think it was a voice from, you know, beyond the grave."

He pokered up. "I'm keeping an open mind."

"You do that. Were you able to dig up any old transmissions?"

He held up a second disc. "Dug them out, last two weeks. You're going to find lots of grease. Guy was working it, trying to pump up some financing. Same on the home unit. Some calls out for food, a couple to a licensed companion service. Couple more back and forth to some place called Bygones."

"Yeah, I'm going to check that out. Looks like he was selling off his stuff."

"You know, he probably had some original art from his grandfather's era. Music posters, photographs, memorabilia."

Considering, Eve cocked her head. "Enough to buy Number Twelve, then finance the rehab?"

"You never know what people'll pay. Got your finger pointed at anyone?"

"Talked to one of his exes, and a son. They don't pop for me, but I'm keeping an open mind. Going through some business associates, potential backers, other exes. No current lady friend, or recently dumped, that I can find. Fact is, the guy comes off as a little sleazy, a little slippery, but mostly harmless. A fuck-up who talked big. Got no motive at this point, except a mysterious something he may or may not have taken with him to Number Twelve."

She eased back. "Big guy. He was a big guy. Easy for a woman to take him down if she's got access to a gun, reasonable knowledge of how it works. Second ex-wife is the kind who holds a grudge, hence my open mind. I've got Peabody trying to run the weapon."

"The thing is," Peabody told her, "it's really old. A hundred years back, a handgun didn't have to be registered on purchase, not in every state, and depending on how it was bought. This one's definitely from the Hop Hopkins/ Bobbie Bray era. They discontinued this model in the Nineteen-eighties. I've got the list of owners with collector's licenses in the state of New York who own that make and model, but . . ."

"It's not going to be there. Not when it was deliberately planted on the scene. The killer wanted it found, identified. Lab comes through, we should know tomorrow if the same gun was used to kill Hopkins and our surprise guest."

She considered for a moment, then pushed away from her desk. "Okay, I'm going to go by the lab, give them a little kick in the ass."

"Always entertaining."

"Yeah, I make my own fun. After, I'm going by this collectibles place, scope it out. It's uptown, so I'll work from home after. I've got Feeney's list of transmissions. You want to take that? Check out the calls, the callers?"

"I'm your girl."

★ ★ ★

Dick Berenski, the chief lab tech, was known as Dickhead for good reason. But besides being one, he was also a genius in his field. Generally, Eve handled him with bribes, insults or outright threats. But with her current case, none were necessary.

"Dallas!" He all but sang her name.

"Don't grin at me like that." She gave a little shudder. "It's scary."

"You've brought me not one but two beauties. I'm going to be writing these up for the trade journals and be the fair-haired boy for the next ten freaking years."

"Just tell me what you've got."

He scooted on his stool, and tapped his long, skinny fingers over a comp screen. He continued to grin out of his strangely egg-shaped head.

"Got my bone guy working with Morris with me running the show. You got yourself a female, between the age of twenty and twenty-five. Bobbie Bray was twenty twenty-three when she poofed. Caucasian, five-foot-five, about a hundred and fifteen pounds, same height and weight on Bobbie's ID at the time of her disappearance. Broken tibia, about the age of twelve. Healed well. Gonna wanna see if we can access any medical records on Bobbie to match the bone break. Got my forensic sculptor working on the face. Bobbie Bray, son of a bitch."

"Another fan."

"Shit yeah. That skirt was *hot*. Got your cause of death, single gunshot wound to the forehead. Spent bullet retrieved from inside the skull matches the caliber used on your other vic. Ballistics confirms both were fired from the weapon recovered from the scene. Same gun used, about eighty-five years apart. It's beautiful."

"I bet the killer thinks so, too."

Sarcasm flew over Dickhead like a puffy white cloud in a sunny blue sky. "Weapon was cleaned and oiled. Really shined it up. But . . ."

He grinned again, tapped again. "What you're looking at here is dust. Brick dust, drywall dust. Samples the sweepers took from the secondary crime scene. And here? Traces of dust found inside the weapon. Perfect match."

"Indicating that the gun was bricked up with the body."

"Guess Bobbie got tired of haunting the place and decided to take a more active role."

And that, Eve determined, didn't even warrant sarcasm as a response. "Shoot the reports to my home and office units, copy to Peabody's. Your sculptor gets an image, I want to see it."

She headed out again, pulling out her 'link as it beeped. "Dallas."

"Arrest any ghosts lately?"

"No. And I'm not planning on it. Why aren't you in a meeting about world domination?"

"Just stepped out," Roarke told her. "My curiosity's been nipping at me all day. Any leads?"

"Leads might be a strong word. I have avenues. I'm heading to one now. The vic was selling off his stuff —

antique popular culture stuff, I gather — to some place uptown. I'm going to check it out."

"What's the address?"

"Why?"

"I'll meet you. I'll be your expert consultant on antiques and popular culture. You can pay my fee with food and sex."

"It's going to be pizza, and I think I've got a long line to credit on the sex."

But she gave him the address.

After ending the transmission, she called the collectibles shop to tell the proprietor to stay open and available. On a hunch, she asked if they carried any Bobbie Bray memorabilia.

And was assured they had the most extensive collection in the city.

Interesting.

# CHAPTER
# FOUR

He beat her there, and was being served coffee and fawning attention by a young, elegant redhead in a slick black suit.

Eve couldn't blame the woman. Roarke was ridiculously handsome, and could, if it served him, ooze charm like pheromones. It seemed to suit him now as he had the redhead flushed and fluttering as she offered cookies with the coffee.

Eve figured she'd benefit from Roarke's charisma herself. She hardly ever got cookies on the job.

"Ah, here's the lieutenant now. Lieutenant Dallas, this is Maeve Buchanan, our hostess, and the daughter of the proprietor."

"Is the proprietor here?"

"My wife. Straight to business. Coffee, darling?"

"Sure. This is some place."

"We're very happy with it," Maeve agreed.

It was pretty, bright — like their hostess — and charmingly organized. Nothing at all like the cluttered junk heap Eve had expected. Art and posters lined the walls, but in a way she supposed someone might arrange them in their home if they were crazy enough to want things everywhere.

Still, tables, display cabinets, shining shelves held memorabilia in a way that escaped the jumbled, crowded stocking style many shops of its kind were victim to. Music was playing unobtrusively — something full of instruments and certainly not of the current era. It added an easy appeal.

"Please, have a seat," Maeve invited. "Or browse if you like. My father's just in the back office. He's on the 'link with London."

"Late for business over there," Eve commented.

"Yes. Private collector. Most of our business is from or to private collections." Maeve swept a wave of that pretty red hair back from her face. "Is there anything I can do for you in the meantime?"

"You've bought a number of pieces over the last several months from Radcliff C. Hopkins."

"Mr Hopkins, of course. Nineteen-sixties through Eighties primarily. We acquired a number of pieces from him. Is there a problem?"

"For Hopkins there is. He was killed last night."

"Oh!" Her cheery, personal-service smile flashed into shock. "Killed? Oh my God."

"Media's run reports on it through the day."

"I . . . I hadn't heard." Maeve's hands were pressed to her cheeks, and her round blue eyes were wide. "We've been open since ten. We don't keep any current screen shows or radio on in the shop. Spoils the . . . the timeless ambiance. My father's going to be so upset."

"They were friends?"

"Friendly, certainly. I don't know what to say. He was in only a few weeks ago. How did he die?"

"The details are confidential." *For the moment*, Eve thought. There were always leaks and the media couldn't wait to soak them up, wring them dry. "I can tell you he was murdered."

Maeve had a redhead's complexion, and her already pale skin went bone white. "Murdered? This is horrible. It's —" She turned as a door in the back opened.

The man who came out was tall and thin, with the red hair he'd passed to his daughter dusted with a little silver. He had eyes of quiet green, and a smile of greeting ready. It faded when he saw his daughter's face.

"Maeve? What's the matter? Is there a problem?"

"Daddy. Mr Hopkins, he's been murdered."

He gripped his daughter's arm, and those quiet eyes skimmed from Roarke to Eve and back again. "Rad Hopkins?"

"That's right." Eve held out her badge. "I'm Lieutenant Dallas. You and Mr Hopkins had business?"

"Yes. Yes. My God, this is such a shock. Was it a burglary?"

"Why would you ask?"

"His collection. He had a very extensive collection of antique art."

"You bought a good chunk of that collection."

"Bits and pieces. Excellent bits and pieces." He rubbed his daughter's shoulder and drew her down to the arm of the chair as he sat. The gesture seemed to help both of them compose themselves.

"I was hoping to eventually do a complete appraisal and give him a bid on the whole of it. But he was . . ."

He pushed at his hair and smiled. "He was canny. Held me off, and whet my appetite with those bits."

"What do you know about Number Twelve?"

"Number Twelve?" He looked blank for a moment, then shook his head. "Sorry, I'm feeling muddled by all this. Urban legend. Haunted. Some say by Hop Hopkins's ghost, others by Bobbie Bray's. Others still say both, or any number of celebrities from that era. Bad luck building, though I admit I'm always on the lookout for something from its heyday that can be authenticated. Rad managed to acquire the building a few months ago, bring it back into his family."

"Do you know how it got out of his family?"

"Ah, I think Rad told me it was sold off when he was a boy. His father inherited it when his grandfather died. Tragically, a drug overdose. And it was Rad's plan to bring it back to its former glory, such as it was."

"He talked about it all the time," Maeve added. "Whenever he came in. Now he'll never . . . It's so sad."

"To be frank," Buchanan continued, "I think he might have overreached a bit. A huge undertaking, which is why he found it necessary — in my opinion — to sell some of his artwork and memorabilia. And because I have a number of contacts in the business who might have been helpful when and if he was ready to outfit the club, it was a good, symbiotic relationship. I'm sorry this happened."

"When was the last time you had contact with him?"

"Just last week. I joined him for a drink, at his invitation. That would be . . ." He closed his eyes a moment, held up a finger. "Wednesday. Wednesday evening of last week. I knew he was going to try to persuade me, again, to invest in this club of his. It's just not the sort of thing I do, but he's a good client, and we were friendly."

When he sighed, Maeve covered his hand with hers. "So I met with him. He was so excited. He told me he was ready to begin the rehab again, seriously this time. He projected opening next summer."

"But you turned him down, investment-wise."

"I did, but he took it well. To be frank again, I did a bit of research when he first approached me months ago. Nothing thrives in that building. Owners and backers go bankrupt or worse. I couldn't see this being any different."

"True enough," Roarke confirmed. "The owners before Hopkins had plans for a small, exclusive spa with restaurant and retail. The buyer fell, broke both his legs while doing a run-through with the architect. His brother and co-buyer were brutally mugged just outside the building. Then his accountant ran off with his wife, taking the bulk of his portfolio."

"Bad luck happens," Eve said flatly. "Could you tell me where you were last night, between midnight and three?"

"Are we suspects?" Maeve's eyes rounded. "Oh my God."

"It's just information. The more I have, the more I have."

"I was out — a date — until about eleven."

"Eleven-fifteen," Buchanan said. "I heard you come in."

"Daddy . . ." Maeve rolled her eyes. "He waits up. I'm twenty-four and he still waits up."

"I was reading in bed." But her father smiled, a little sheepishly. "Maeve came in, and I . . . well . . ." He sent another look toward his daughter. "I went down about midnight and checked security. I know, I know," he said before Maeve could speak. "You always set it if you come in after I'm in bed, but I feel better doing that last round. I went to bed after that. Maeve was already in her room. We had breakfast together about eight this morning, then we were here at nine-thirty. We open at ten."

"Thanks. Is it all right if we take a look around?"

"Absolutely. Please. If you have any questions — if there's anything we can do . . ." Buchanan lifted his hands. "I've never dealt with anything like this, so I'm not sure what we can or should do."

"Just stay available," Eve told him. "And contact me at Central if anything comes to mind. For now, maybe you can point me toward what you've got on Bobbie Bray."

"Oh, we have quite a collection. Actually, one of my favorites is a portrait we bought from Rad a few months ago. This way." Buchanan turned to lead them through the main showroom. "It was done from the photograph taken for her first album cover. Hop — the first Hopkins — had it painted, and it hung in the apartment he kept over Number Twelve. Rumor is he held long conversations with it after she disappeared. Of course, he ingested all manner of hallucinogens. Here she is. Stunning, isn't it?"

The portrait was perhaps eighteen by twenty inches, in a horizontal pose. Bobbie reclined over a bed spread with vivid pink and mounded with white pillows.

Eve saw a woman with wild yards of curling blond hair. There were two sparkling diamond clips glinting in the masses of it. Her eyes were the green of new spring leaves, and a single tear — bright as the diamonds — spilled down her cheek. It was the face of a doomed angel — lovely rather than beautiful, full of tragedy and pathos.

She wore thin, filmy white, and between the breasts was a deep red stain in the blurred shape of a heart.

"The album was *Bleeding Heart*, for the title track. She won three Grammys for it."

"She was twenty-two," Maeve put in. "Two years younger than me. Less than two years later, she vanished without a trace."

There was a trace, Eve thought. There always was, even if it was nearly a century coming to light.

Outside, Eve dug her hands into her pockets. The sky had stopped spitting out nasty stuff, but the wind had picked up. She was pretty sure she'd left her watch cap in her office.

"Everybody's got an alibi, nobody's got a motive. Yet. I think I'm going to go back to the scene, take another look around."

"Then you can fill me in with what must be a multitude of missing details on the way. I had my car taken home," Roarke continued when she frowned at him. "So I could get a lift with my lovely wife."

"You were just hoping to get a look at Number Twelve."

"And hope springs. Want me to drive?"

When she slid behind the wheel, she tapped her fingers on it. "What's something like that painting going to go for on the open market?"

"To the right collector? Sky would be the limit. But I'd say a million wouldn't be out of the park."

"A million? For a painting of a dead woman. What's wrong with people? Top transaction in the vic's account from Bygones was a quarter of that. Why'd Hopkins sell so cheap?"

"Scrambling for capital. Bird in the hand's worth a great deal more than a painting on the wall."

"Yeah, there's that. Buchanan had to know he was getting bargain basement there."

"So why kill the golden goose?"

"Exactly. But it's weird to me neither of them had heard by this time that Hopkins bought it at Number Twelve. They eat breakfast at eight? No media reports while you're scoping out the pickings on the AutoChef or pulling on your pants?"

"Not everyone turns on the news."

"Maybe not. And nobody pops in today, mentions it? Nobody say, 'Hey! Did you hear about that Hopkins guy? Number Twelve got another one.' Just doesn't sit level for me." Then she shrugged, pulled away from the curb.

"Hit the lab before this. The same gun that killed Hopkins killed the as yet unidentified female whose remains were found behind the wall at Number Twelve."

"Fascinating."

"Weapon was bricked up with her. Killer must have found her, and it. Cleaned the weapon. You see those, the hair jewelry, she had on in the picture? Recovered at the scene, also clean and shiny. One by the window which the killer likely used to escape, one left with the bones."

"Someone wants to make sure the remains are identified. Do you doubt it's her?"

"No, I don't doubt it's her. I don't doubt Hop Hopkins put a bullet in her brain, then got handy with brick and mortar. I don't know why. I don't know why someone used that same gun on Hop's grandson eighty-five years later."

"But you think there's a connection. A personal one."

"Had to reload to put the bullet in the brain. That's extremely cold. Guy's dead, or next to it. But you reload, roll the body over, press the barrel down hard enough to scorch the skin and leave an imprint of the barrel, and give him one last hit. Fucking cold."

# CHAPTER
## FIVE

Eve gave him details on the drive. She could, with Roarke, run them through like a checklist, and it always lined them up in her mind. In addition, he always seemed to know something or someone that might fill in a few of the gaps.

"So, did you ever do business with Hopkins?"

"No. He had a reputation for being generous with the bullshit, and often short on results."

"Big plans, small action," Eve concluded.

"That would be it. Harmless, by all accounts. Not the sort to con the widow and orphans out of the rent money, but not above talking them out of a portion of it with a view to getting rich quick."

"He cheated on his wives, and recently squeezed five hundred out of the son he abandoned."

"Harmless doesn't always mean moral or admirable. I made a few calls — curiosity," he explained. "To people who like to buy and sell real estate."

"Which includes yourself."

"Most definitely. From what I'm told the bottom dropped out of Twelve for Hopkins only a couple of weeks after he'd signed the papers on it. He was in fairly deep — purchase price, legal fees, architects and designers, construction crew, and so on. He'd done a lot of tap dancing to get as far as he did, and was running out of steam. He'd done some probing around — more legal fees — to see if he could wrangle having the property condemned, and get back some of his investment. Tried to wrangle some money from various federal agencies, historic societies. He played all the angles and had some success. A couple of small grants. Not nearly enough, not for his rather ambitious vision."

"What kind of money we talking, for the building and the vision?"

"Oh, easily a hundred and fifty million. He'd barely scratched the surface when he must have realized he couldn't make it without more capital. Then, word is, a few days ago, he pushed the green light again. Claimed Number Twelve was moving forward."

"I'm waiting on the lab to see if they can pinpoint when that wall was taken down. Could be talking days." Her fingers tapped out a rhythm on the wheel as she considered. "Hopkins finds the body. You get a wealth of publicity out of something like that. Maybe a vid deal, book deals. A guy with an entrepreneurial mindset, he could think of all kinds of ways to rake it in over those bones."

"He could," Roarke agreed. "But wouldn't the first question be how he knew where to look?"

"Or how his killer knew."

"Hop killed her," she began as she hunted for parking. "Argument, drug-induced, whatever. Bricks up the body, which takes some doing. Guy liked cocaine. That'll keep you revved for a few hours. Has to cover up the brick, put things back into reasonable shape. I'm trying to access the police reports from back then. It hasn't been easy so far. But anyway, no possible way the cops just missed a brand new section of wall, so he paid them off or blackmailed them."

"Corrupt cops? I'm stunned. I'm shocked."

"Shut up. Hop goes over the edge — guilt, drugs, fear of discovery. Goes hermit. Guy locks himself up with a body on the other side of the wall, he's going to go pretty buggy. Wouldn't surprise me if he wrote something down, told someone about it. If cops were involved, they knew or suspected something. The killer, or Hopkins, does some homework, pokes around. Gets lucky, or unlucky as the case may be."

"It takes eight and a half decades to get lucky?"

"Place gets a rep," Eve said as they walked from the car toward Number Twelve. "Bray gets legend status. People report seeing her, talking to her. A lot of those people, and others, figure she just took off 'cause she couldn't handle the pressure of her own success. Hop has enough juice to keep people out of the apartment during his lifetime. By then, there're murmurs of curses and hauntings, and that just grows as time passes. A couple of people have some bad luck, and nobody much wants to play in Number Twelve anymore."

"More than a couple." Roarke frowned at the door as Eve uncoded the police seal. "The building just squats here, and everyone who's tried to disturb it, for whatever reason, ends up paying a price."

"It's brick and wood and glass."

"Brick and wood and glass form structure, not spirit."

She raised her brows at him. "Want to wait in the car, Sally?"

"Now you shut up." He nudged her aside to walk in first.

She turned on the lights, took out her flashlight for good measure. "Hopkins was between those iron stairs and the bar." She moved across the room, positioned herself by the stairs. "From the angles, the killer was here. I'm seeing he got here first, comes down when Hopkins walks in. Hopkins still had his coat on, his gloves, a muffler. Cold in here, sure, but a man's going to probably pull off his gloves, unwrap his scarf, maybe unbutton his coat when he's inside. You just do."

Understanding his wife, Roarke moved into what he thought had been Hopkins's standing position. "Unless you don't have the chance."

"Killer comes down. He'd told Hopkins to bring something, and Hopkins walks in empty-handed. Could have been small — pocket-sized — but why would the killer shoot him so quickly, and with such rage, if he'd cooperated?"

"The man liked to spin the wheels. If he came empty, he may have thought he could work a deal."

"So when he starts the whole 'Let's talk about this', the killer snaps. Shoots him. Chest, leg. Four shots from the front. Vic goes down, tries to crawl, killer keeps firing, moving toward the target. Leg, back, shoulder. Eight shots. Full clip for that model. Reloads, shoves the body over, leans down. Looks Hopkins right in the eyes. Eyes are dead, but he looks into them when he pulls the trigger the last time. He wants to see his face — as much as he needs to echo the head shot on Bray, he needs to see the face, the eyes, when he puts that last bullet in."

She crossed over, following what she thought was the killer's route as she'd spoken. "Could have gone out the front. But he chooses to go back upstairs."

Now she turned, started up. "Could have taken the weapon, thrown it in the river. We'd never have found it. Wants us to find it. Wants us to know. Cops didn't put Hop in the system. Why should we do anything about his grandson? Took care of that himself. Payment made. But he wants us to know, everyone to know, that Bobbie's been avenged at last."

She stopped in front of the open section of wall. "'Look what he did to her. Put a bullet in that young, tragic face, silenced that voice. Ended her life when it was just getting started. Then he put a wall up, locked her away from the world. She's free now. I set her free.'"

"She'll be more famous, more infamous, than ever. Her fans will make a shrine out of this place. Heap flowers and tokens outside, stand in the cold with candles for vigils. And, to add a cynical note, there'll be Bobbie Bray merchandising through the roof. Fortunes will be made out of this."

Eve turned back to Roarke. "Damn right, they will. Hopkins would have known that. He'd have had visions of money falling on him from the sky. Number Twelve wouldn't just be a club, it would be a freaking cathedral. And he's got the main attraction. Fame and fortune off her bones. You bet your ass. Killer's not going to tolerate that. 'You think you can use her? You think I'd let you?'"

"Most who'd have known her personally, had a relationship with her, would be dead now. Or elderly."

"Don't have to be young to pull a trigger." But she frowned at the cut in the wall. "But you'd have to be pretty spry to handle the tools to do this. I just don't think this part was Hopkins's doing. Nothing in his financials to indicate he'd bought or rented the tools that could handle this. And he doesn't strike me as the type who'd be able to do this tidy a job with them. Not on his own. And the killer had the gun, the hair clips. The killer opened this grave."

The cold was sudden and intense, as if a door had been flung open to an ice floe, and through that frigid air drifted a raw and haunting voice.

*In my dark there is no dawn, there is no light in my world since you've been gone. I thought my love would stand the test, but now my heart bleeds from my breast.*

Even as Eve drew her weapon, the voice rose, with a hard, throbbing pump of bass and drums behind it. She rushed out to the level overlooking the main club.

The voice continued to rise, seemed to fill the building. Under it, over it, were voices, cheers and whistles. For an instant, she thought she could smell a heavy mix of perfume, sweat, smoke.

"Somebody's messing with us," she murmured.

Before she could swing toward the stairs to investigate, there was a shout from the nearly gutted apartment above. A woman's voice called out:

"No. Jesus, Hop. Don't!"

There was the explosion of a shot and a distinct thud.

Keeping her weapon out, she vaulted up the stairs again with Roarke. At the doorway, his hand clamped over her shoulder.

"Holy Mother of God. Do you see?"

She told herself it was a shadow — a trick of the poor light, the dust. But for an instant there seemed to be a woman, her mass of curling blond hair falling over her shoulders, standing in front of the open section of wall. And for an instant, it seemed her eyes looked straight into Eve's.

Then there was nothing but a cold, empty room.

"You saw her," Roarke insisted as Eve crawled around behind the wall.

"I saw shadows. Maybe an image. If I saw an image, it was because someone put it there. Just like someone flipped some switch to put on that music. Got some electronics set up somewhere. Triggered by remote, most likely."

He crouched down. Eve's hair, face, hands were all coated with dust and debris. "You felt that cold."

"So, he dropped the temp in here. He's putting on a show, that's what he's doing. Circus time. So the cop goes back and reports spooky happenings, apparitions. Bull-*shit*!"

She swiped at her filthy face as she crawled out. "Hopkins left debts. His son is beneficiary of basically nada. Building's no-man's-land until it goes up to public auction. Keep the curse crap going, keep the price down. Snap it up cheaper than dirt."

"With what's happened here, discovering the body here, that could go exactly the opposite way. It could drive the price up."

"That happens, you bet your ass someone's going to have some document claiming they were partners with Hopkins. Maybe I was wrong about it being personal. Maybe it's been profit all along."

"You weren't wrong. You know you weren't. But you're sitting there, in a fairly disgusting state, I might add, trying to turn it around so you don't have to admit you've seen a ghost."

"I saw what some mope wants me to believe is a ghost and he apparently pulled one over on you, ace."

"I know electronic imagery when I see it." The faintest edge of irritation flickered into his eyes at her tone. "I know what I saw, what I heard, what I felt. Murder was done here, then adding to it, the insult, the callousness of what was done after."

He glanced back into the narrow opening, toward the former location of the long-imprisoned bones. And now there was a hint of pity in his eyes as well. "All while claiming to be so concerned, so upset, offering rewards for her safe return, or for substantiated proof she was alive and well. All that while she was moldering behind the wall he'd built to hide her.

"If her body never left here, why should her spirit?"

54

"Because —" With a shake of her head, Eve scattered dust. "Her body's not here now. So shouldn't she be haunting the morgue?"

"This place has been home to her for a long time, hasn't it?" *Pragmatism*, he thought, *thy name is Eve.* Then he took out a handkerchief, used it to rub the worst of the dust and grime from her face.

"Homemade crypts aren't what I'd call home, sweet home," she retorted. "And you know what? Ghosts don't clean guns or shoot them. I've got a DB in the morgue. And I'm ordering the sweepers, with a contingent from EDD in here tomorrow. They're going to take this place apart."

She brushed some of the dirt from her shirt and pants before picking up her coat. "I want a shower."

"I want you to have a shower, too."

As they went downstairs, she called in the order for two units to search Number Twelve for electronic devices. If she thought she heard a woman's husky laugh just before she closed and secured the door, Eve ignored it.

# CHAPTER
# SIX

When she'd showered and pulled on warm, comfortable sweats, Eve gave another thought to pizza. She figured she could down a slice or two at her desk while she worked.

She was headed toward the office she kept at home when she heard Bobbie Bray's voice, gritting out her signature song.

*Broken, battered, bleeding, and still I'm begging, pleading*

*Come back. Come back and heal my heart*

*Come back. Come back and heal my heart*

With her own heart thudding, Eve covered the rest of the distance at a dash. Except for the fat cat, Galahad, snoring in her sleep chair, her office was empty.

Then she narrowed her eyes at the open door that joined her office to Roarke's. She found him at his desk, with the title track beginning its play again through the speakers of his entertainment unit.

"You trying to wig me out?"

"No." He smiled a little. "Did I?" When she gave him a stony stare, he shrugged. "I wanted to get better acquainted with our ghost. She was born in Louisville, Kentucky, and according to this biography, left home at sixteen to migrate to Haight-Ashbury, as many of her generation did. She sang in some clubs, primarily for food or a place to sleep, drifted around, joined a band called Luv — that's L-U-V — where she stood out like a rose among weeds, apparently. Did some backup singing for one or two important artists of the time, then met Hopkins in Los Angeles."

"Bad luck for her. Can you turn that off?"

"Music off," he ordered, and Bobbie's voice stopped. "She bothers you," Roarke realized. "Why is that?"

"She doesn't bother me." *The correct term*, Eve thought, *would be she creeps me.* But damned if she was going to fall into the accepted pattern on Number Twelve, or Bobbie Bray.

"She's part of my investigation — and a secondary vic, even though she was killed a half century before I was born. She's mine now, like Hopkins is mine. But she's always part of the motive."

"And as such, I'd think you'd want to know all you could about her."

"I do, and I will. But I don't have to hear her singing." It was too sad, Eve admitted to herself. And too spooky. "I'm going to order up some pizza. You want in on that?"

"All right." Roarke rose to follow her into the kitchen attached to her office. "She was twenty when Hop scooped her up. He was forty-three. Still, it was two years before her album came out — which he produced, allegedly hand-picking every song. She did perform during that period, exclusively in Hopkins's venues."

"So he ran her."

"All but owned her, from the sound of it. Young, naive girl — at least from a business standpoint, and from a generation and culture that prided itself on not being bound by property and possessions. Older, canny, experienced man, who discovered her, romanced her, and most certainly fed any appetite she might have had for illegal substances."

"She'd been on her own for five years." Eve debated for about five seconds on pepperoni and went for it. "Naive doesn't wash for me."

"But then you're not a sentimental fan or biographer. Still, I'd lean toward the naivete when it came to contracts, royalties, business and finance. And Hopkins was a pro. He stood as her agent, her manager, her producer."

"But she's the talent," Eve reasoned and snagged some napkins. "She's got the youth, the looks. Maybe her culture or whatever said pooh-pooh to big piles of money, but if she's bringing it in, getting the shine from it, she's going to start to want more."

"Agreed. She left him for a few months in 1972, just dropped off the radar. Which is one of the reasons, I'd assume, he got away with her murder three years later. She'd taken off once, why not again?"

He stepped out to choose a wine from the rack behind a wall panel. "When she came back, it was full-court press professionally, with a continual round of parties, clubs, drugs, sex. Her album hit, and big, with her touring internationally for six months. More sex, more drugs, and three Grammys. Her next album was in the works when she disappeared."

"Hop must've gotten a percentage of her earnings." Eve brought the pizza in, dumped it and plates on her desk.

"As her manager and producer, he'd have gotten a hefty one."

"Stupid to kill the goose."

"Passion plus drugs can equal extreme stupidity."

"Smart enough to cover it up, and keep it covered for eighty-five years. So his grandson ends up paying for it. Why? My vic wasn't even born when this went down. If it's revenge . . ."

"Served very cold," Roarke said as he poured wine.

"The killer has a connection with the older crime, the older players. Financial, emotional, physical. Maybe all three."

She lifted up a slice, tugged at the strings of cheese, expertly looping them up and over the triangle.

"If it's financial," she continued, "who stands to gain? The son inherits, but he's alibied and there isn't a hell of a lot to scoop once the debts are offset. So maybe something of value, something the killer wanted Hopkins to bring to Number Twelve. But if it's a straight give-me-what-I-want/deserve, why set the scene? Why put on that show for us tonight?"

When Roarke said nothing, Eve chewed contemplatively on her slice. "You don't seriously believe that was some ghostly visitation? Grab a little corner of reality."

"Do you seriously believe your killer has been dogging that building, its owners, for eight and a half decades? What makes that more logical than a restless, angry spirit?"

"Because dead people don't get angry. They're dead." She picked up her wine. "It's my job to get pissed for them."

Roarke studied her over his own glass, his gaze thoughtful, seeking. "Then there's nothing after? As close as you've been to the dead, you don't see something after?"

"I don't know what I see." This sort of conversation always made her uncomfortable, somehow sticky along the skin. "Because you don't see it — if it's there to see — until you're dead. But I don't believe the dead go all *whoooo*, or start singing. The original Hopkins paid an investigation off, this killer wants to weird one off. It's not going to work."

"Consider the possibility," he suggested. "Bobbie Bray's spirit wants her revenge as much as you want justice. It's a powerful desire, on both parts."

"That's not a possible possibility."

"Closed-minded."

"Rational," she corrected, with some heat now. "Jesus, Roarke, she's bones. Why now then? Why here and now? How'd she manage to get someone — flesh and blood — to do the descendent of her killer? If Hop Hopkins *was* her killer — which hasn't yet been proven."

"Maybe she was waiting for you to prove it."

"Oh yeah, *that's* rational. She's been hanging around, waiting for the right murder cop to come along. Listen, I've got the reality of a dead body, an antique and banned weapon used in a previous crime. I've got no discernible motive and a media circus waiting to happen. I can't take the time to wonder and worry about the disposition of a woman who's been dead eighty-five years. You want to waste your time playing with ghosts, be my guest. But I've got serious work on my plate."

"Fine then, since it pisses you off, I'll just leave you to your serious work while I go waste my time."

She scowled at him when he got up and carried his glass of wine with him to his office. And she cursed under her breath when he closed the door behind him.

"Great, fine, fabulous. Now I've got a ghost causing marital discord. Just makes it all perfect."

She shoved away from her desk to set up the case board she used at home. Logic was what was needed here, she told herself. Logic, cop sense, facts and evidence.

Must be that Irish in Roarke's blood that tugged him into the fanciful. Who knew he'd head that way?

But her way was straight, narrow and rational.

Two murders, one weapon. Connection. Two murders, one location, second connection. Second vic, blood descendent of suspected killer in first murder. Connect those dots, too, she thought as she worked.

So, okay, she couldn't set the first murder aside. She'd use it.

Logic and evidence dictated that both victims knew their killer. The first appeared to be a crime of passion, likely enhanced by illegal substances. Maybe Bray cheated on Hop. Or wanted to break things off professionally and/or personally. She could have had something on him, threatened exposure.

Had to be an act of passion, heat of the moment. Hop had the money, the means. If he'd planned to kill Bray, why would he have done it in his own apartment?

But the second murder was a deliberate act. The killer lured the victim to the scene, had the weapon. Had, in all likelihood discovered the previous body. The killing had been an act of rage as well as deliberation.

"Always meant to kill him, didn't you?" she murmured as she studied the crime scene photos on her board. "Wanted whatever you wanted first — but whether or not you got it, he was a dead man. What did she mean to you?"

She studied the photos of Bobbie Bray.

Obsessed fan? Not out of the realm, she thought, but low on her list.

"Computer, run probability with evidence currently on active file. What is probability that the killers of Bray, Bobbie and Hopkins, Radcliff C. are linked?"

Working . . .

Absently, Eve picked up her wine, sipping as she worked various scenarios through her head.

Task complete. Probability is eighty-two-point-three . . .

Reasonably strong, Eve mused, and decided to take it one step further. "What is the probability that the killer of Hopkins, Radcliff C. is linked with the first victim, Bray, Bobbie?"

Working . . .

*Family member,* Eve thought. *Close friend, lover. Bray would be, what . . . Damn math,* she cursed as she calculated. *Bray would be around about one-oh-nine if she'd lived. People lived longer now than they did in the mid-twentieth. So a lover or tight friend isn't out of the realm either.*

But she couldn't see a centenarian, even a spry one, cutting through that brick.

Task complete. Probability is ninety-four-point-one that there is a connection between the first victim and the second killer . . .

"Yeah, that's what I think. And you know what else? Blood's the closest connection. So who did Bobbie leave behind? Computer, list all family members of first victim. Display on wall screen one."

Working . . . Display complete.

Parents and older brother deceased, Eve noted. A younger sister, age eighty-eight, living in Scottsdale Care Center, Arizona. Young for a care center, Eve mused, and made a note to find out what the sister's medical condition was.

Bobbie would have had a niece and nephew had she lived, and a couple of grandnieces and nephews.

Worth checking into, Eve decided, and began a standard run on all living relations.

While the computer worked, she set up a secondary task and took a closer look at Hopkins.

"Big starter," she said aloud. "Little finisher."

There were dozens of projects begun, abandoned. Failed. Now and then he'd hit, at least enough to keep the wolves from the door, set up the next project.

Failed marriages, ignored offspring. No criminal on any former spouse or offspring.

But you had to start somewhere, she figured.

She went back to the board. Diamond hair clips. Bray had worn them for her first album cover — possibly a gift from Hop. Most likely. The scene told Eve it was likely Bray had been wearing them when she'd been killed, or at least when she'd been bricked up.

But the killer hadn't taken them as a souvenir. Not a fan, just didn't play. The killer had shined them up and left them behind.

"She was a diamond," Eve murmured. "She shined. Is that what you're telling me? Here's the gun he used to kill her, and here's where I found it. He never paid and payment needed to be made. Is that the message?"

She circled the boards, studied the runs when the computer displayed them. There were a couple of decent possibilities among Bobbie's descendents.

They'd all have to be interviewed, she decided.

*One of them contacts Hopkins,* she speculated. *Maybe even tries to buy the building but can't come up with the scratch. Has to get access though, to uncover the body. How was access gained?*

Money. Hopkins needed backers. Maybe charged his murderer a fee to tour Number Twelve. Get in once, you can get in again.

*How'd you find the body? How did you know?*

What did she have here? she asked herself. Younger sister in a care facility. Niece a data drone. Nephew deceased — Urban War fatality. Grandniece middle-management in sales, grandnephew an insurance salesman. Rank and file, no big successes, no big failures.

Ordinary.

Nothing flashy. Nobody managed to cash in on Bobbie's fame and fortune, or her untimely death.

Nobody, she mused, except Hopkins. That would be a pisser, wouldn't it? Your daughter, sister, aunt is a dead cult figure, but you've got to do the thirty-five hours a week to get by. And the grandson of the bastard who killed her is trying to rake it in. You're scraping by, getting old and . . .

"Wait a minute, wait a minute. Serenity Bray, age eighty-eight. Twenty-two years younger than Bobbie. Not a sister. A daughter."

She swung to the adjoining door, shoved it open. "Bobbie had a kid. Not a sister. The timing's right. She had a kid."

Roarke merely lifted an eyebrow. "Yes. Serenity Bray Massey, currently in Scottsdale in a full-care nursing facility. I've got that."

"Showoff. She had a kid, and the timing makes it most likely Hop's. There's no record of a child. No reports from that time of her pregnancy. But she separated from him for several months, which would coincide with the last few months of her pregnancy and the birth."

"After which, it would seem, she gave the child to her own mother. Who then moved her family to a ranch outside Scottsdale, and Bobbie went back to Hop, and her previous lifestyle. I've found some speculation that during her period of estrangement from Hop she went into rehab and seclusion. Interviews and articles from the time have her clean and sober when she returned to the scene, then backsliding, I suppose you could say, within weeks."

He angled his head. "I thought you were leaving Bobbie to me."

"The ghost part's yours. The dead part's mine."

# CHAPTER
# SEVEN

They were into their second year of marriage, and being a trained observer, Eve knew when he was irritated with her. It seemed stupid, just *stupid* to have a fight or the undercurrent of one over something as ridiculous as ghosts.

Still, she brooded over it another moment, on the verge of stupidity. Then she huffed out a breath.

"Look," she began.

After a pause, he sat back. "I'm looking."

"What I'm getting at is . . . shit. Shit." She paced to his window, to the doorway, turned around again.

Rules of marriage — and hell, one of the benefits of it, she admitted — were that she could say to him what she might even find hard to say to herself.

"I have to live with so many of them." There was anger in her over it, and a kind of grief she could never fully explain. "They don't always go away when you close the case, never go away if you leave a crack in it. I got a freaking army of dead in my head."

"Whom you've defended," he reminded her. "Stood over, stood for."

"Yeah, well, that doesn't mean they're going to say 'Thanks, pal,' then shuffle off the mortal whatever."

"That would be coil — and they've already done the shuffle before you get there."

"Exactly. Dead. But they still have faces and voices and pain, at least in my head. I don't need to think about one wifting around sending me messages from beyond. It's too much, that's all. It's too much if I have to start wondering if there's some spirit hovering over my shoulder to make sure I do the job."

"All right."

"That's it?"

"Darling Eve," he said with the easy patience he could pull out and baffle her with at the oddest times. "Haven't we already proven that you and I don't have to stand on exactly the same spot on every issue? And wouldn't it be boring if we did?"

"Maybe." Tension oozed back out of her. "I guess. I just never expected you'd take something like this and run with it."

"Then perhaps I shouldn't tell you that if I die first, I'm planning to come back to see you naked as often as possible."

Her lips twitched, as he'd intended them to. "I'll be old, with my tits hanging to my waist."

"You don't have enough tit to hang that low."

She pursed her lips, looked down as if to check. "Gotta point. So are we good now?"

"We may be, if you come over here and kiss me. In payment for the insult."

She rolled her eyes. "Nothing's free around here." But she skirted the desk, leaned down to touch her lips to his.

The moment she did, he yanked her down into his lap. She'd seen it coming — she knew him too well not to — but was in the mood to indulge him.

"If you think I'm playing bimbo secretary and horny exec —"

"There were actually a few insults," he interrupted. "And you've reminded me that you're going to get old eventually. I should take advantage of your youth and vitality, and see you naked now."

"I'm not getting naked. Hey! Hey!"

"*Feel* you naked then," he amended, as his hands were already under her sweatshirt and on her breasts. "Good things, small packages."

"Oh yeah? Is that what I should say about your equipment?"

"Insult upon insult." Laughing, he slid his hand around to her back to hold her more firmly in place. "You have a lot of apologizing to do."

"Then I guess I'd better get started."

She put some punch into the kiss, swinging around to straddle him. It would take some agility as well as vitality to pull off a serious apology in his desk chair, but she thought she was up to the job.

He made her feel so many things, all of them vital and immediate. The hunger, the humor, the love, the lust. She could taste his heat for her, his greed for her as his mouth ravished hers. Her own body filled with that same heat and hunger as he tugged at her clothes.

Here was his life — in this complicated woman. Not just the long, alluring length of her, but the mind and spirit inside the form. She could excite and frustrate, charm and annoy — and all there was of her somehow managed to fit against him, and make him complete.

Now she surrounded him, shifting that body, using those quick hands, then taking him inside her with a long, low purr of satisfaction. They took each other, finished each other, and then the purr was a laughing groan.

"I think that squares us," she managed.

"You may even have some credit."

For a moment, she curled in, rested her head on his shoulder. "Ghosts probably can't screw around in a desk chair."

"Unlikely."

"It's tough being dead."

At eight-fifteen in the morning, Eve was in her office at Central scowling at the latest sweeper and EDD reports.

"Nothing. They can't find anything. No sign of electronic surveillance, holographic paraphernalia, audio, video. Zilch."

"Could be it's telling you that you had a paranormal experience last night."

Eve spared one bland look for Peabody. "Paranormal my ass."

"Cases have been documented, Dallas."

"Fruitcakes have been documented, too. It's going to be a family member. That's where we push. That and whatever Hopkins may or may not have had in his possession that his killer wanted. Start with the family members. Let's eliminate any with solid alibis. We'll fan out from there."

She glanced at her desk as her 'link beeped — again — and, scanning the readout, sneered. "Another reporter. We're not feeding the hounds on this one until so ordered. Screen all your incomings. If you get cornered, straight no comment, investigation is active and ongoing. Period."

"Got that. Dallas, what was it like last night? Skin-crawly or wow?"

Eve started to snap, then blew out a breath. "Skin-crawly, then annoying that some jerk had played with me and made my skin crawl for a minute."

"But kind of frigid, too, right? Ghost of Bobbie Bray serenading you."

"If I believed it was the ghost of anyone, I'd say it was feeling more pissy than entertaining. What someone wants us to think is we're not welcome at Number Twelve. Trying to scare us off. I've got Feeney's notes on the report from EDD. He says a couple of his boys heard singing. Another swears he felt something pat his ass. Same sort of deal from the sweepers. Mass hysteria."

"Digging in, I found out two of the previous owners tried exorcisms. Hired priests, psychics, parapsychologists, that kind of deal. Nothing worked."

"Gee, mumbo didn't get rid of the jumbo? Why doesn't that surprise me? Get on the 'link, start checking alibis."

Eve took her share, eliminated two, and ended up tagging Serenity Massey's daughter in the woman's Scottsdale home.

"It's not even seven in the morning."

"I'm sorry, Ms Sawyer."

"Not even seven," the woman said testily, "and I've already had three calls from reporters, and another from the head nurse at my mother's care center. Do you know a reporter tried to get to her? She has severe dementia — can barely remember me when I go see her — and some idiot reporter tries to get through to interview her over Bobbie Bray. My mother didn't even *know* her."

"Does your mother know she was Bobbie Bray's daughter?"

The woman's thin, tired face went blank. But it was there in her eyes, clear as glass. "What did you say?"

"She knows, then — certainly you do."

"I'm not going to have my mother harassed, not by reporters, not by the police."

"I don't intend to harass your mother. Why don't you tell me when and how she found out she was Bobbie's daughter, not her sister."

"I don't know." Ms Sawyer rubbed her hands over her face. "She hasn't been well for a long time, a very long time. Even when I was a child . . ." She dropped her hands now and looked more than tired. She looked ill. "Lieutenant, is this necessary?"

"I've got two murders. Both of them relatives of yours. You tell me."

"I don't think of the Hopkins family as relatives. Why would I? I'm sorry that man was killed because it's dredged all this up. I've been careful to separate myself and my own family from the Bobbie phenomenon.

Check, why don't you? I've never given an interview, never agreed to one or sought one out."

"Why? It's a rich pool, from what I can tell."

"Because I wanted *normal*. I'm entitled to it, and so are my kids. My mother was always frail. Delicate, mind and body. I'm not, and I've made damn sure to keep me and mine out of that whirlpool. If it leaks out that I'm Bobbie's granddaughter instead of a grandniece, they'll hound me."

"I can't promise to keep it quiet, I can only promise you that I won't be giving interviews on that area of the investigation. I won't give out your name or the names of your family members."

"Good for you," Sawyer said dully. "They're already out."

"Then it won't hurt you to answer some questions. How did your mother find out about her parentage?"

"She told me — my brother and me — that she found letters Bobbie had written. Bobbie's mother kept them. She wrote asking how her baby was doing, called my mother by name. Her Serenity she called her, as if she was a state of mind instead of a child who needed her mother."

The bitterness in the words told Eve she wasn't talking to one of Bobbie Bray's fans.

"Said she was sorry she'd messed up again. My mother claimed Bobbie said she was going back into rehab, that she was leaving Hop, the whole scene. She was going to get clean and come back for her daughter. Of course, she never came back. My mother was convinced Hop had killed her, or had her killed."

"What do you think?"

"Sure, maybe." The words were the equivalent of a shrug. "Or maybe she took off to Bimini to sell seashells by the seashore. Maybe she went back to San Francisco and jumped off the Golden Gate Bridge. I don't know, and frankly don't much care."

Sawyer let out a long sigh, pressed her fingers to her eyes. "She wasn't, and isn't, part of my world. But she all but became my mother's world. Mom swore Bobbie's ghost used to visit her, talk to her. I think it's part of the reason, this obsession, that she's been plagued by emotional and mental problems as long as I can remember. When my brother was killed in the Urbans, it just snapped her. He was her favorite."

"Do you have the letters?"

"No. That Hopkins man, he tracked my mother down. I was in college, my brother was overseas, so that was, God, about thirty years ago. He talked her out of nearly everything she had that was Bobbie's or pertained to her. Original recordings, letters, diaries, photographs. He said he was going to open some sort of museum in California. Nothing ever came of it. My brother came home and found out. He was furious. He and my mother had a horrible fight, one they never had a chance to reconcile. Now he's gone and she might as well be. I don't want to be Bobbie Bray's legacy. I just want to live my life."

Eve ended the transmission, tipped back in her chair. She was betting the letters were what the killer had been after.

With Peabody she went back to Hopkins's apartment for another thorough search.

"Letters Bobbie wrote that confirm a child she had with Hop. Letters or some sort of document or recording from Hop that eventually led his grandson to Serenity Massey. Something that explosive and therefore valuable," she said to her partner. "I bet he had a secure hidey-hole. Security box, vault. We'll start a search of bank boxes under his name or likely aliases."

"Maybe he took them with him and the killer already has them."

"I don't think so. The doorman said he walked out empty-handed. Something like that, figuring the value, he's going to want a briefcase, a portfolio. Guy liked accessories — good suit, shoes, antique watch — why miss a trick with something that earns one? But . . . he was hunting up money. Maybe he sold them, or at least dangled them."

"Bygones?"

"Worth a trip."

At the door, Eve paused, turned to study the apartment again. There'd be no ghosts here, she thought. Nothing here but stale air, stale dreams.

Legacies, she thought as she closed the door. Hopkins left one of unfulfilled ambitions, which to her mind carried on the one left by his father.

Bobbie Bray's granddaughter had worked hard to shut her own heritage out, to live simply. Didn't want to be Bobbie Bray's legacy, Eve recalled.

Who could blame her? Or anyone else for that matter.

"If you're handed crap and disappointment — *inherited* it," Eve amended, "what do you do?"

"Depends, I guess." Peabody frowned as they headed down. "You could wallow in it and curse your ancestors, or shovel yourself out of it."

"Yeah. You could try to shine it up into gold and live the high life — like Hopkins. Obsess over it like Bray's daughter. Or you could shut the door on it and walk away. Like Bray's granddaughter."

"Okay. And?"

"There's more than one way to shut a door. You drive," Eve said when they were outside.

"Drive? Me? It's not even my birthday!"

"Drive, Peabody." In the passenger seat, Eve took out her PPC and brought up John Massey's military ID data. She cocked her head as she studied the photo.

He'd been young, fresh-faced. A little soft around the mouth, she mused, a little guileless in the eyes. She didn't see either of his grandparents in him, but she saw something else.

Inherited traits, she thought. Legacies.

Using the dash 'link, she contacted police artist Detective Yancy.

"Got a quick one for you," she told him. "I'm going to shoot you an ID photo. I need you to age it for me."

# CHAPTER
# EIGHT

Eve had Peabody stop at the bank Hopkins had used for his loan on Number Twelve. But there was no safety deposit box listed under his name, or Bray's, or any combination.

To Peabody's disappointment, Eve took the wheel when they left the bank.

She couldn't justify asking Roarke to do the search for a safety deposit box, though it passed through her mind. He could no doubt pinpoint one, if one was there to be pinpointed, faster than she could. Even faster than EDD. But she couldn't term it a matter of life and death.

Just a matter of irritation.

She put in a request to Feeney to assign the task to EDD ace, and Peabody's heartthrob, Ian McNab while she and Peabody headed back to Bygones.

"McNab will be so completely jazzed about this." Smiling — as if even saying his name put a dopey look on her face — Peabody wiggled in the passenger seat. "Looking for a ghost and all that."

"He's looking for a bank box."

"Well yeah, but in a roundabout way, it's about Bobbie Bray and the ghost thereof. Number Twelve."

"Stop saying that." Eve wanted to grip her own hair and yank, but her hands were currently busy on the wheel. She used those hands to whip around a farting maxibus with a few layers of paint to spare. "I'm going to write an order forbidding anyone within ten feet of me from saying *Number Twelve* in that — what is it — awed whisper."

"But you just gotta. Did you know there are all these books, and there are vids, based on Number Twelve, and Bobbie and the whole deal from back then? I did some research. McNab and I downloaded one of the vids last night. It was kind of hokey, but still. And we're working the case. Maybe they'll make a vid of *that* — you know, like they're going to do one of the Icove case. Completely uptown. We'll be famous, and —"

Eve stopped at a light, turned her body slowly so she faced her partner. "You even breathe that thought, I'll choke you until your eyes pop right out of their sockets, then plop into your open gasping mouth where you'll swallow them whole. And choke to death on your own eyeballs."

"Well, jeez."

"Think about it, think carefully, before you breathe again."

Peabody hunched in her seat and kept her breathing to a minimum.

When they found the shop closed and locked, they detoured to the home address on record.

Maeve opened the door of the three-level brownstone. "Lieutenant, Detective."

"Closed down shop, Ms Buchanan?"

"For a day or two." She pushed at her hair. Eve watched the movement, the play of light on the striking red. "We were overrun yesterday, only about an hour after you left. Oh, come in, please. I'm a little flustered this morning."

"Overrun?" Eve repeated as she stepped into a long, narrow hallway brightened by stained glass windows that let in the winter sun.

"Customers, and most of them looking for bargains. Or wanting to gawk over the Bobbie Bray collection." Maeve, dressed in loose white pants, a soft white sweater and white half boots led the way through a wide doorway into a spacious parlor.

Tidy, Eve thought, but not fussy. Antiques — she knew how to recognize the real thing, as Roarke had a penchant for them. Deep cushions in rich colors, old rugs, what looked to be old black-and-white photographs in pewter frames adorning the walls.

No gel cushions, no mood screen, no entertainment unit in sight. Old-world stuff, Eve decided, very much like their place of business.

"Please, have a seat. I've got tea or coffee."

"Don't worry about it," Eve told her. "Your father's here?"

"Yes, up in the office. We're working from here, at least for today. We're buried in inquiries for our Bray collection, and we can handle those from home."

She moved around the room, turning on lamps with colored shades. "Normally, we'd love the walk-in traffic at the shop, but not when it's a circus parade. With only the two of us, we just couldn't handle it. We have a lot of easily lifted merchandise."

"How about letters?"

"Letters?"

"You carry that sort of thing? Letters, diaries, journals?"

"We absolutely do. On Bobbie again?" Maeve walked back to sit on the edge of a chair, crossed her legs. "We have what's been authenticated as a letter she wrote to a friend she'd made in San Francisco — ah . . . 1968. Two notebooks containing original lyrics for songs she'd written. There may be more, but those spring to mind."

"How about letters to family, from her New York years?"

"I don't think so, but I can check the inventory. Or just ask my father," she added with a quick smile. "He's got the entire inventory in his head, I swear. I don't know how he does it."

"Maybe you could ask him if he could spare us a few minutes."

"Absolutely."

When she hesitated, Eve primed her. "Is there something else, something you remember?"

"Actually, I've been sort of wrestling with this. I don't think it makes any difference. I didn't want to say anything in front of my father." She glanced toward the doorway, then tugged lightly — nervously, Eve thought — on one of the sparkling silver hoops she wore in her ears. "But . . . well, Mr Hopkins — Rad — he sort of hit on me. Flirted, you know. Asked me out to dinner, or drinks. He said I could be a model, and he could set me up with a photographer who'd do my portfolio at a discount."

She flushed, the color rising pink into her cheeks, and cleared her throat. "That kind of thing."

"And did you? Have drinks, dinner, a photo session?"

"No." She flushed a little deeper. "I know when I'm getting a line. He was old enough to be my father, and well, not really my type. I won't say there wasn't something appealing about him. Really, he could be charming. And it wasn't nasty, if you know what I mean. I don't want you to think . . ."

She waved a hand in the air. "It was all sort of friendly and foolish. I might have even been tempted, just for the fun. But I've been seeing someone, and it's turning into a thing. I didn't want to mess that up. And frankly, my father wouldn't have liked it."

"Because?"

"The age difference for one, and the type of man Rad was. Opportunistic, multiple marriages. Plus, he was a client and that can get sticky. Anyway." Maeve let out a long, relieved breath. "It was bothering me that I didn't mention it to you, and that you might hear about it and think I was hiding something."

"Appreciate that."

"I'll go get my father," she said as she rose. "You're sure you won't have coffee? Tea? It's bitter out there today."

"I wouldn't mind either," Peabody put in. "Dealer's choice. The lieutenant's coffee — always black."

"Fine. I'll be back in a few. Make yourselves comfortable."

"She was a little embarrassed about the Hopkins thing. She wanted to serve us something," Peabody said when Maeve left the room. "Makes it easier for her."

"Whatever floats." Eve got to her feet, wandered the room. It had a settled, family feel about it, with a thin sheen of class. The photos were arty black-and-whites of cities — old-timey stuff. She was frowning over one when Buchanan came in. Like his daughter, he was wearing at-home clothes. And still managed to look dignified in a blue sweater and gray pants.

"Ladies. What can I do for you?"

"You have a beautiful home, Mr Buchanan," Peabody began. "Some wonderful old pieces. Lieutenant, it makes me wonder if Roarke's ever bought anything from Mr Buchanan."

"Roarke?" Buchanan gave Peabody a puzzled look. "He has acquired a few pieces from us. You're not saying he's a suspect in this."

"No. He's Lieutenant Dallas's husband."

"Of course, I forgot for a moment." He shifted his gaze to Eve with a smile. "My business keeps me so much in the past, current events sometimes pass me by."

"I bet. And speaking of the past," Eve continued, "we're interested in any letters, journals, diaries you might have that pertain to Bobbie Bray."

"That's a name I've heard countless times today. Maeve might have told you that's why we decided to work from home. And here she is now."

Maeve wheeled in a cart holding china pots and cups.

"Just what we need. I've put the 'links on auto," her father told her. "We can take a short break. Letters." He took a seat while Maeve poured coffee and tea. "We do have a few she wrote to friends in San Francisco in 1968 and 1969. And one of our prizes is a workbook containing drafts of some of her song lyrics. It could, in a way, be considered a kind of diary as well. She wrote down some of her thoughts in it, or notes to herself. Little reminders. I've fielded countless inquiries about just that this morning. Including one from a Cliff Gill."

"Hopkins's son?"

"So he said. He was very upset, nearly incoherent really." Buchanan patted Maeve's hand when she passed him a cup. "Understandable under the circumstances."

"And he was looking specifically for letters?" Eve asked.

"He said his father had mentioned letters, a bombshell as he put it. Mr Gill understood his father and I had done business and hoped I might know what it was about. I think he hopes to clear his family name."

"You going to help him with that?"

"I don't see how." Buchanan spread his hands. "Nothing I have pertains."

"If there was something that pertained, or correspondence written near the time of her disappearance, would you know about it?"

He pursed his lips in thought. "I can certainly put out feelers. There are always rumors, of course. Several

**83**

years ago someone tried to auction off what they claimed was a letter written by Bobbie two years after her disappearance. It was a forgery, and there was quite a scandal."

"There have been photos, too," Maeve added. "Purportedly taken of Bobbie after she went missing. None have ever been authenticated."

"Exactly." Buchanan nodded. "So substantiating the rumors and the claims, well, that's a different matter. Do you know of correspondence from that time, Lieutenant?"

"I've got a source claiming there was some."

"Really." His eyes brightened. "If they're authentic, acquiring them would be quite a coup."

"Were you name-dropping, Peabody?" Eve gave her partner a mild look as she slid behind the wheel.

"Roarke's done business there before, and you guys went there together. But he doesn't mention Roarke at all. And being in business, I figured Buchanan would keep track of his more well-heeled clients, you know, and should've made an immediate connection."

"Yeah, you'd think. Plausible reason he didn't."

"You'd wondered, too."

"I wonder all kinds of things. Let's wonder our way over to talk to Cliff Gill."

Like Bygones, the dance school was locked up tight. But as Fanny Gill lived in the apartment overhead, it was a short trip.

Cliff answered looking flushed and harassed. "Thank God! I was about to contact you."

"About?"

"We had to close the school." He took a quick look up and down the narrow hallway then gestured them inside. "I had to give my mother a soother."

"Because?"

"Oh, this is a horrible mess. I'm having a Bloody Mary."

Unlike the Buchanan brownstone, Fanny's apartment was full of bright, clashing colors, a lot of filmy fabrics and chrome. Artistic funk, Eve supposed. It was seriously lived in to the point of messy.

Cliff was looking pretty lived-in himself, Eve noted. He hadn't shaved, and it looked like he'd slept in the sweats he was wearing. Shadows dogged his eyes.

"I stayed the night here," he began as he stood in the adjoining kitchen pouring vodka. "People came into the studio yesterday afternoon, some of them saying horrible things. Or they'd just call, leaving horrible, nasty transmissions. I've turned her 'links off. She just can't take any more."

He added enough tomato juice and Tabasco to turn the vodka muddy red, then took a quick gulp. "Apparently we're being painted with the same brush as my grandfather. Spawn of Satan." He took another long drink, then blushed. "I'm sorry. I'm sorry, what can I get you?"

"We're fine," Eve told him. "Mr Gill, have you been threatened?"

"With everything from eternal damnation to public flogging. My mother doesn't deserve this, Lieutenant. She's done nothing but choose poorly in the husband department, which she rectified. At least I carry the same blood as Hopkins." His mouth went grim. "If you think along those lines."

"Do you?"

"I don't know what I think any more." He came back into the living area, dropped onto a candy-pink sofa heaped with fluffy pillows. "At least I know what to feel now. Rage, and a little terror."

"Did you report any of the threats?"

"She asked me not to." He closed his eyes, seemed to gather some tattered rags of composure. "She's embarrassed and angry. Or she started out that way. She didn't want to make a big deal about it. But it just kept up. She handles things, my mother, she doesn't fall apart. But this has just knocked her flat. She's afraid we'll lose the school, all the publicity, the scandal. She's worked so hard, and now this."

"I want you to make a copy of any of the transmissions regarding this. We'll take care of it."

"Okay. Okay." He scooped his fingers through his disordered hair. "That's the right thing to do, isn't it? I'm just not thinking straight. I can't see what I should do."

"You contacted the owner of a shop called Bygones. Care to tell me why?"

"Bygones? Oh, oh, right. Mr Buchanan. My father sold him some memorabilia. I think maybe Buchanan was one of the backers on Number Twelve. My father mentioned him when I gave him the five hundred. Said something like Bygones may be Bygones, but he wouldn't be nickel-and-diming it any more. How he'd pay me back the five or ten times over because he was about to hit the jackpot."

"Any specific jackpot?"

"He talked a lot, my father. Bragged, actually, and a lot of the bragging was just hot air. But he said he'd been holding onto an ace in the hole, waiting for the right time. It was coming up."

"What was his hole card?"

"Can't say he actually had one." Cliff heaved out a breath. "Honestly, I didn't really listen because it was the same old, same old to me. And I wanted to get him moving before my mother got wind of the loan. But he said something about letters Bobbie Bray had written. A bombshell, he said, that was going to give Number Twelve just the push he needed. I didn't pay much attention at the time because he was mostly full of crap."

He winced now, drank again. "Hell of a thing to say about your dead father, huh?"

"His being dead doesn't make him more of a father to you, Mr Gill," Peabody said gently.

Cliff's eyes went damp for a moment. "Guess not. Well, when all this started happening, I remembered how he talked about these letters, and I thought maybe he'd sold them to Bygones. Maybe there was something in them that would clear my grandfather. Something, I don't know. Maybe she committed suicide and he panicked."

He lowered his head, rubbed the heel of his hand in the center of his brow as if to push away some pain. "I don't even care, or wouldn't, except for what's falling down from it on my mother. I don't know what I expected Mr Buchanan to do. I was desperate."

"Did your father give you any indication of the contents of the letters?" Eve asked. "The timing of them?"

"Not really, no. At the time I thought it was just saving face because I was giving him money. Probably all it was. Buchanan said he hadn't bought any letters from my father, but I could come in and look at what he had. Waste of time, I guess. But he was nice about it — Buchanan, I mean. Sympathetic."

"Have you discussed this with your mother at all?" Peabody asked him.

"No, and I won't." Any grief seemed to burn away as anger covered his face. "It's a terrible thing to say, but by dying my father's given her more trouble than he has since she divorced him. I'm not going to add to it. Chasing a wild goose anyway." He frowned into his glass. "I have to make some arrangements for — for the body. Cremation, I guess. I know it's cold, but I'm not going to have any sort of service or memorial. I'm not going to drag this out. We just have to get through this."

"Mr Gill —"

"Cliff," he said to Eve with a weak smile. "You should call me Cliff since I'm dumping all my problems on you."

"Cliff. Do you know if your father kept a safety deposit box?"

"He wouldn't have told me. We didn't see each other much. I don't know what he'd have kept in one. I got a call from some lawyer this morning. Said my father'd made a will, and I'd inherit. I asked him to ballpark it, and the gist was when it all shakes out, I'll be lucky to have enough credits to buy a soy dog at a corner cart."

"I guess you were hoping for better," Peabody commented.

Cliff let out a short, humorless laugh. "Hoping for better with Rad Hopkins would be another waste of time."

# CHAPTER
# NINE

"You have to feel for the guy." Peabody bundled her scarf around her neck as they walked back outside.

"We'll pass off the copy of his 'link calls to a couple of burly uniforms, have them knock on some doors and issue some stern warnings. About all we can do there for now. We're going back to Central. I want a quick consult with Mira, and you can update the Commander."

"*Me?*" Peabody's voice hit squeak. "Alone? Myself?"

"I expect Commander Whitney would be present as you're updating him."

"But you do the updates."

"Today you're doing it. He's going to want to set up a media conference," Eve added as she got into their vehicle. "Hold him off."

"Oh my God."

"Twenty-four hours. Make it stick," Eve added and pulled out into traffic as Peabody sat pale and speechless beside her.

Mira was the top profiler attached to the NYPSD for good reason. Her status kept her in high demand and made Eve's request for a consult without appointment similar to trying to squeeze her head through the eye of a needle that was already threaded.

She had a headache when she'd finished battling Mira's admin, but she got her ten minutes.

"You ought to give her a whip and a chain," Eve commented when she stepped into Mira's office. "Not that she needs one."

"You always manage to get past her. Have a seat."

"No thanks, I'll make it fast."

Mira settled behind her desk. She was a sleek, lovely woman who favored pretty suits. Today's was power red and worn with pearls.

"This would be pertaining to Number Twelve," Mira began. "Two murders, nearly a hundred years apart. Your consults are rarely routine. Bobbie Bray."

"You, too? People say that name like she's a deity."

"Do they?" Mira eased back in her chair, her blue eyes amused. "Apparently my grandmother actually heard her perform at Number Twelve in the early Nineteen-seventies. She claimed she exchanged an intimate sexual favor with the bouncer for the price of admission. My grandmother was a wild woman."

"Huh."

"And my parents are huge fans, so I grew up hearing that voice, that music. It's confirmed then? They were her remains?"

"Lab's forensic sculptor's putting her money on it as of this morning. I've got the facial image she reconstructed from the skull, and it looks like Bray."

"May I see?"

"I've got it in the file." Eve gave Mira the computer codes, then shifted so she, too, could watch the image come on-screen.

The lovely, tragic face, the deep-set eyes, the full, pouty lips somehow radiated both youth and trouble.

"Yes," Mira murmured. "It certainly looks like her. Something so sad and worn about her, despite her age."

"Living on drugs, booze and sex tends to make you sad and worn."

"I suppose it does. You don't feel for her?"

Eve realized she should have expected the question from Mira. Feelings were the order of the day in that office. "I feel for anyone who gets a bullet in the brain — then has their body closed up in a wall. She deserves justice for that — deserves it for the cops who looked the other way. But she chose the life she led to that point. So looking sad and worn at twenty-couple? No, I can't say I feel for that."

"A different age," Mira said, studying Eve as she'd studied the image on screen. "My grandmother always said you had to be there. I doubt Bobbie would have understood you and the choices you've made any more than you do her and hers."

Mira flicked the screen off. "Is there more to substantiate identity?"

"The bones we recovered had a broken left tibia, which corresponds with a documented childhood injury on Bray. We extracted DNA, and I've got a sample of a relative's on its way to the lab. It's going to confirm."

"A tragic waste. All that talent snuffed out."

"She didn't live what you could call a careful life."

"The most interesting people rarely do." Mira angled her head. "You certainly don't."

"Mine's about the job. Hers was about getting stoned and screwing around, best I can tell."

Now Mira raised a brow. "Not only don't you feel for her, you don't think you'd have liked her."

"Can't imagine we'd have had much in common, but that's not the issue. She had a kid."

"What? I've never heard that."

"She kept it locked. Likelihood is it was Hop Hopkins's offspring, though it's possible she got knocked up on the side. Either way, she went off, had the kid, dumped it on her mother. Sent money so the family could relocate — up the scale some. Mother passed the kid off as her own."

"And you find that deplorable, on all counts."

Irritation shadowed Eve's face, very briefly. "That's not the issue either. Female child eventually discovered her heritage through letters Bray allegedly wrote home. The ones shortly before her death, again allegedly, claimed that she was planning to clean up her act — again — and come back for the kid. This is hearsay. The daughter relayed it to her two children. Purportedly the letters and other items were sold, years ago, to Radcliff C. Hopkins — the last."

"Connections within connections. And this, you believe goes to motive."

"You know how Hopkins was killed?"

"The walls are buzzing with it. Violent, specific, personal — and somehow tidy."

"Yeah." It was always satisfying to have your instincts confirmed. "The last shot. Here's what he did to her.

There's control there, an agenda fulfilled, even through the rage."

"Let me see if I understand. You suspect that a descendent of Bobbie Bray killed a descendent of Hopkins to avenge her murder."

"That's a chunk of it, buttonholed. According to Bray's granddaughter, the murder, the abandonment, the obsession ruined her mother's health. Series of breakdowns."

"You suspect the granddaughter?"

"No, she's covered. She's got two offspring herself, but I can't place them in New York during the time in question."

"Who does that leave you?"

"There was a grandson, reported killed in action during the Urbans."

"He had children?"

"None on record. He was pretty young, only seventeen. Lied about his age when he joined up — a lot of people did back then. Oddly enough, he was reported killed here in New York."

Pursing her lips, Mira considered. "As you're one of the most pragmatic women I know, I find it hard to believe you're theorizing that a ghost killed your victim to avenge yet another ghost."

"Flesh and blood pulled the trigger. I've got Yancy aging the military ID. The Urban Wars were a chaotic time, and the last months of them here in New York were confusing from a military standpoint. Wouldn't be hard, would it, for a young man, one who'd already lied about his age to enlist in the Home Force, to put his

94

official ID on a mangled body and vanish? War's never what you think it's going to be. It's not heroic and adventurous. He could've deserted."

"The history of mental illness in the family — on both sides — the horrors of war, the guilt of abandoning his duty. It would make quite a powder keg. Your killer is purposeful, specific to his goal, would have some knowledge of firearms. Rumor is the victim was shot nine times — the weapon itself is a symbol — and there were no stray bullets found on scene."

"He hit nine out of nine, so he had some knowledge of handguns, or some really good luck. In addition, he had to reload for the ninth shot."

"Ah. The others were the rage, that slippery hold on control. The last, a signature. He's accomplished what he meant to do. There may be more, of course, but he has his eye for an eye, and he has the object of his obsession back in the light."

"Yeah." Eve nodded. "I'm thinking that matters here."

"With Bobbie's remains found, identified, and her killer identified — at least in the media — he's fulfilled his obligation. If the killer is the grandson — or connected to the grandson, as even if he did die in the Urbans, it's certainly possible to have produced an offspring at seventeen — he or she knows how to blend."

"Likely to just keep blending," Eve added.

"Most likely. I don't believe your killer will seek the spotlight. He doesn't need acknowledgment. He'll slide back into his routine, and essentially vanish again."

"I think I know where to find him."

★ ★ ★

"Yancy does good work." Eve held the photos of John Massey — youth and maturity — side-by-side.

"He does," Roarke agreed. "As do you, Lieutenant. I doubt I'd have looked at the boy and seen the man."

"It's about legacies. Redheads ran in Bray's family. Her father, her daughter. Her grandson."

"And Yancy's work indicates he's alive and living in New York."

"Yeah. But even with this I've got nothing but instinct and theories. There's no evidence linking the suspect to the crime."

"You've closed a case on a murder that happened decades before you were born," Roarke reminded her. "Now you're greedy."

"My current suspect did most of the work there. Discovered the body, unearthed it, led me to it. The rest was basically lab and leg work. Since the perpetrator of that crime is long dead, there's nothing to do but mark the file and do the media announcement."

"Not very satisfying for you."

"Not when somebody kills a surrogate figuring that evens things up. And plays games with me. So it's our turn to play." Eve shifted in the limo. She felt ridiculous riding around in the big black boat.

But no one would expect Roarke to ride the subway, or even use a common Rapid Cab. Perception was part of the game.

"I can't send you in wired," she added. "Never get a warrant for eyes or ears with what I've got. You know what to say, right? How to play it?"

**96**

"Lieutenant, have a little faith."

"I got all there is. Okay," she added, ducking down a little to check out the window when the limo glided to the curb. "Showtime. I'll be cruising around in this thing, making sure the rest of this little play is on schedule."

"One question. Can you be sure your suspect will hit his cue in this play of yours?"

"Nothing's a given, but I'm going with the odds on this. Obsession's a powerful motivator. The killer is obsessed with Bray, with Number Twelve — and there's a sense of theatrics there. Another legacy, I'd say. We dangle the bait, he's going to bite."

"I'll do my best to dangle it provocatively."

"Good luck."

"Give us a kiss then."

"That's what you said last night, and look what happened." But she gave him a quick one. When he slipped out of the limo, she pulled out her 'link to check on the rest of the game.

Roarke walked into Bygones looking like a man with plenty of money and an eye to spend it as he liked. He gave Maeve an easy smile and a warm handshake. "Ms Buchanan? I appreciate you opening for me this afternoon. Well, it's nearly evening, isn't it?"

"We're happy to oblige. My father will be right out. Would you like a glass of wine? I have a very nice cabernet breathing."

"I'd love one. I've met your father, though it's been three or four years, I suppose, since we've done business."

"I'd have been in college. He mentioned you'd bought a particularly fine Georgian sideboard and a set of china, among other things."

"He has an excellent memory."

"He never forgets a thing." She offered the wine she'd poured, then gestured to a silver tray of fruit and cheese. "Would you like to sit? If you'd rather browse, I can point you in a direction, or show you whatever you'd like. My father has the piece you inquired about. He wanted to make sure it was properly cleaned before he showed it to you."

"I'll just wait then, if you'll join me." As he sat, he glanced toward the portrait of Bobbie on the far wall. "It's actually Bobbie Bray who put me in mind to come here."

"Oh? There's always interest in her and her memorabilia, but in the last day it's piqued."

"I imagine." He shifted as he spoke so he could scan the black-and-white photographs Eve had told him about. And two, as she'd mentioned, were desert landscapes. "Just as I imagine it won't ebb any time soon," he continued. "Certainly not with the publicity that will be generated from the case finally being solved."

Maeve's hands went very still for a moment. "It's certain then?"

"I have an inside source, as you might suspect. Yes, it's certain. She's been found, after all these years. And the evidence proves it was Hopkins who hid her body."

"Horrible. I — Daddy." She got to her feet as Buchanan came into the shop. He carried a velvet case. "You remember Roarke."

"I certainly do. It's good to see you again." They shook hands, sat. "Difficult circumstances when you were here recently with your wife."

"Yes. Terrible. I was just telling your daughter that they've confirmed the identity of the remains found at Number Twelve, and found Hopkins's — the first's — fingerprints on the inside of the wall, on several of the bricks."

"There's no doubt any longer then."

"Hardly a wonder he went mad, locking himself up in that building, knowing what he'd done, and that she was behind that wall, where he'd put her. A bit of 'The Telltale Heart,' really."

Keeping it conversational, Roarke settled back with his drink. "Still, it's fascinating, isn't it? Time and distance tend to give that sort of brutality an allure. No one can speak of anything else. And here I am, just as bad. Is that the necklace?"

"Oh, yes. Yes." Buchanan unsnapped the case, folded back the velvet leaves. "Charming, isn't it? All those little beads are hand-strung. I can't substantiate that Bobbie made it herself, though that's the story. But it was worn by her to the Grammy Awards, then given by her to one of her entourage. I was able to acquire it just last year."

"Very pretty." Roarke held up the multistrand necklace. The beads were of various sizes, shapes, colors, but strung in a way that showed the craftsman had a clever eye. "I think Eve might like this. A memento of Bobbie, since she's the one who's finally bringing her some sense of justice."

"Can there be, really?" Eyes downcast, Maeve murmured it. "After all this time?"

"For my cop, justice walks hand-in-hand with truth. She won't let the truth stay buried, as Bobbie was." He held up the beads again. "I'm hoping to take her away for a quick tropical holiday, and this sort of thing would suit the tropics, wouldn't it?"

"After this New York weather?" Maeve said with a laugh as she lifted her gaze once more. "The tropics would suit anything."

"With our schedules it's difficult to get away. I'm hoping we can find that window. Though with what they've found today, it may take a bit longer."

"They found something else?" Buchanan asked.

"Mmm. Something about a bank box, letters, and so on. And apparently something the former Hopkins recorded during his hermitage. My wife said he spoke of a small vault in Number Twelve, also walled in. Hopkins must have been very busy. They're looking for it, but it's a good-sized building. It may take days."

"A vault." Maeve breathed the words. "I wonder what's in it."

"More truth?" But Buchanan's voice was strained now. "Or the ramblings of a madman, one who'd already killed?"

"Perhaps both," Roarke suggested. "I know my wife's hoping for something that will lead her to Rad Hopkins's killer. The truth, and justice for him as well."

He laid the necklace on the velvet. "I'm very interested in this piece." Roarke sipped his wine. "Shall we negotiate?"

# CHAPTER
# TEN

In Number Twelve, Eve stood in the area that had once held a stage. Where there had been sound and light and motion, there was silence, dark and stillness. She could smell dust and a faint whiff of the chemicals the sweepers used on-scene. And could feel nothing but the pervading chill that burned through the brick and mortar of an old building.

Still, the stage was set, she thought. If her hunch was off, she'd have wasted a lot of departmental time, manpower and money. Better that, she decided, than to play into the current media hype that the curse of Number Twelve was still vital, still lethal.

"You've got to admit, it's creepy." Beside Eve, Peabody scanned the club room. There was a lot of white showing in her eyes. "This place gives me the jeebies."

"Keep your jeebies to yourself. We're set. I'm going up to my post."

"You don't have to go up right this minute." Peabody's hand clamped like a bundle of live wires on Eve's wrist. "Seriously. We've got plenty of room on the timetable."

"If you're afraid of the dark, Detective, maybe you should've brought a nice little teddy bear to hold onto."

"Couldn't hurt," Peabody mumbled when Eve pulled free. "You'll stay in contact, right? I mean, communications open? It's practically like you're standing beside me."

Eve only shook her head as she crossed to the stairs. She'd gone through doors with Peabody when death or certainly pain was poised on the other side. She'd crawled through blood with her. And here her usually stalwart partner was squeaking over ghosts.

Her bootsteps echoed against the metal steps — and okay, maybe it was a little creepy. But it wasn't creaking doors and disembodied moans they had to worry about tonight. It was a stone killer who could come for letters from the dead.

There were no letters, of course. None that she knew of, no vault to hide them in. But she had no doubt the prospect of them would lure Rad Hopkins's killer into Number Twelve.

No doubt that killer was descended from Bray and Hopkins. If her hunch didn't pay off tonight, she was going to face a media storm tomorrow — face it either way, she admitted. But she'd rather deal with it with the case closed.

Funny how Bygones had old-timey photos of the desert. Maybe they were Arizona, maybe not, but she was laying her money that they were. There'd been old photos of San Francisco, too, before the quake had given it a good, hard shake. Others of New York during that time period, and of LA. All of Bobbie's haunts.

Coincidence, maybe. But she agreed with one of the detectives in her squad on a case recently closed — a case that also included switched identities.

Coincidences were hooey.

She crossed the second tier, and started up to the old apartment.

Eve didn't doubt Roarke had played his part, and played it well. With the bait he'd dangled, she was gambling that Radcliff C. Hopkins's killer, and Bobbie Bray's murderous descendent, would bite quickly. Would bite tonight.

She took her position where she could keep the windows in view, put her back to the wall. Eve flipped her communications channel to Peabody's unit, and said, "Boo."

"Oh yeah, that's funny. I'm rib-cracking down here."

"When you're finished with your hilarity, we'll do a check. Feeney, you copy?"

"Got your eyes, your ears and the body-heat sensors. No movement."

"You eating a doughnut?"

"What do you need electronic eyes and ears for, you can tell I'm eating a cruller from in there?" There was a slurping sound as Feeney washed down the cruller with coffee. "Roarke bought the team a little something to keep us alert."

"Yeah, he's always buying something." She wished she had a damn cruller. Better, the coffee.

"You should have worn the beads, Lieutenant." Roarke's voice cruised on. "I think they might have appealed to Bobbie."

"Yeah, that's what I need. Baubles and beads. I could use them to —"

"Picking up something," Feeney interrupted.

"I hear it." Eve went silent, and as she focused, the sound — a humming — took on the pattern of a tune, and a female flavor. She drew her weapon.

"Exits and egresses," she murmured to Feeney.

"Undisturbed," he said in her ear. "I've got no motion, no visual, no heat-sensor reading on anything but you and Peabody."

So it was on a timer, Eve decided. An electronic loop EDD had missed.

"Dallas?" Peabody's voice was a frantic hiss. "You read? I see —"

The earpiece went to a waspy buzz. And the air went to ice.

She couldn't stop the chill from streaking up her spine, but no one had to know about it. She might have cursed the glitch in communications and surveillance, but she was too busy watching the amorphous figure drift toward her.

Bobbie Bray wore jeans widely belled from the knees down, slung low at the hips and decorated with flowers that twined up the side of each leg. The filmy white top seemed to float in a breeze. Her hair was a riotous tangle of curls with the glitter of diamond clips. As she walked, as she hummed, she lifted a cigarette to her lips and drew deeply.

For an instant, the sharp scent of tobacco stung the air.

From the way the image moved, Eve decided tobacco wasn't the only thing she'd been smoking. As ghosts went, this one was stoned to the eyeballs.

"You think I'm buying this?" Eve pushed off the wall. But when she started to move forward something struck out at her. Later, she would think it was like being punched with an ice floe.

She shoved herself forward, following the figure into what had been the bedroom area of the apartment.

The figure stopped, as if startled.

*I didn't know you were up here. What's it about? I told you, I'm bookin'. So I packed. Don't give me any more shit, Hop.*

The figure moved as it spoke, mimed pouring something into a glass, drinking. There was weariness in the voice, and the blurriness of drugs.

*Because I'm tired and I'm sick. I'm so fucking messed up. This whole scene is fucked up, and I can't do it anymore. I don't give a shit about my career. That was all you. It's always been all you.*

She turned, stood hipshot and blearily defiant.

*Yeah? Well, maybe I have lapped it up, and now I'm just puking it out. For Christ's sake look at us, Hop. Look at yourself. We're either stoned or strung out. We got a kid. Don't tell me to shut up. I'm sick of myself and I'm sick of you. I will stay straight this time.*

The image flung an arm out as if heaving a glass against the wall.

*I'm not humping some other guy. I'm not signing with another label. I'm done. Don't you get it? I'm done with this, and I'm done with you. You're fucking crazy, Hop. You need help more than I do. Put that down.*

The image threw up its hands now, stumbling back.

*You gotta calm down. You gotta come down. We'll talk about it, okay? I don't have to leave. I'm not lying. I'm not. Oh God. Don't. No. Jesus, Hop. Don't!*

There was a sharp crack as the figure jerked back, then fell. The hole in the center of the forehead leaked blood.

"Hell of a show," Eve said, and her voice sounded hoarse to her own ears. "Hell of a performance."

Eve heard the faint creak behind her, pivoted. Maeve stepped into the room, tears pouring down her cheeks. And a knife gleaming dully in her hand.

"He shot me dead. Dead was better than gone — that's what he said."

Not John Massey, Eve realized. The Bray/Hopkins legacy had gone down another generation.

"You look alive to me, Maeve."

"Bobbie," she corrected. "She's in me. She speaks through me. She is me."

Eve let out a sigh, kept her weapon down at her side. "Oh step back. Ghosts aren't ridiculous enough, now we have to go into possession?"

"And he killed me." Maeve crooned it. "Took my life. He said I was nothing without him, just a junky whore with a lucky set of pipes."

"Harsh," Eve agreed. "I grant you. But it all happened before you were born. And both players are long dead. Why kill Hopkins?"

**106**

"He walled me up." Her eyes gleamed, tears and rage and madness. "He paid off the cops, and they did *nothing*."

"No, he didn't. His grandfather did."

"There's no difference." She turned a slow circle as she spoke, arms out. "He was, I was. He is, I am." Then spun, pointed at Eve with the tip of the knife. "And you, you're no different than the cops who let me rot in there. You're just another pig."

"Nobody pays me off. I finish what I start, and let me tell you something: this stops here."

"It never stops. I can't get out, don't you get it?" Maeve slapped a hand over her lips as if to hold back the gurgle of laughter that ended on a muffled sob. "Every day, every night, it's the same thing. I can't get away from it, and I go round and round and round, just like he wanted."

"Well, I'm going to help you get out of here. And you can spend every day, every night of the rest of your natural life in a cage. Might be a nice padded one in your case."

Maeve smiled now. "You can't stop it. You can't stop me, you can't stop it. 'You're never leaving me.' That's what he said when he was walling me up in there. He made me, that's what he said, and I wasn't going anywhere. Ever. Fucking bastard killed me, cursed me, trapped me. What the hell are you going to do about it?"

"End it. Maeve Buchanan, you're under arrest for the murder of Radcliff Hopkins. You have the right to remain silent —"

"You'll pay for leaving me in there!" Maeve hacked out with the knife she held and missed by a foot.

"Jesus, you fight like a girl." Eve circled with her, watching Maeve's eyes. "I'm not an overweight dumbass, and you don't have a gun this time. So pay attention. Stunner, knife. Stunner always wins. You want a jolt, Maeve?"

"You can't hurt me. Not in this place. I can't be harmed here."

"Wanna bet?" Eve said, and hit Maeve with a low stun when the redhead charged again.

The knife skittered out of Maeve's hand as she fell back, hit hard on her ass. There was another swipe of cold, this time like ice-tipped nails raking Eve's cheek. But she pushed by it, yanking out her restraints as she dragged Maeve's arms behind her back.

Maeve struggled, her body bucking as she gasped out curses. And the cold, whipped by a vicious wind, went straight down to the bone.

"This stops here," Eve repeated, breathless as what felt like frigid fists pounded at her back. "Radcliff C. Hopkins will be charged with murder one in the unlawful death of Bobbie Bray, posthumously. That's my word. Period. Now leave me the hell alone so I can do my job."

Eve hauled Maeve to her feet as the wind began to die. "We're going to toss in breaking and entering and assault on an officer just for fun."

"My name is Bobbie Bray, and you can't touch me. I'm Bobbie Bray, do you hear me? I'm Bobbie Bray."

"Yeah, I hear you." Just as she heard the sudden frantic squawking of voices in her ear and the thunder of footsteps on the stairs.

"I couldn't get to the stairs," Peabody told her. "All of a sudden the place is full of people and music. Talk about jeebies. My communication's down, and I'm trying to push through this wall of bodies. Live bodies — well, not live. I don't know. It's all jumbled."

"We went to the doors soon as communications went down," Feeney added. "Couldn't get through them. Not even your man there with his magic fingers. Then all of a sudden, poof, corn's back, locks open, and we're in. Damned place." Feeney stared at Number Twelve as they stood on the sidewalk. "Ought to be leveled, you ask me. Level the bastard and salt the ground."

"Maeve Buchanan rigged it, that's all. We'll figure out how." That was her story, Eve told herself, and she was sticking with it. "I'm heading in, taking her into interview. She's just whacked enough she may not lawyer up straight off."

"Can I get a lift?"

Eve turned to Roarke. "Yeah, I'll haul you in. Uniforms are transporting the suspect to Central. Peabody, you want to supervise that?"

"On it. Glad to get the hell away from this place."

When he settled in the car beside Eve, Roarke said simply, "Tell me."

"Maeve was probably already inside. We just missed her in the sweep. She had a jammer and a program hidden somewhere."

"Eve."

She huffed out a breath, cursed a little. "If you want to be fanciful or whatever, I had a conversation with a dead woman."

She told him, working hard to be matter-of-fact.

"So it wasn't Maeve who bruised and scratched your face."

"I don't know what it was, but I know this is going to be wrapped, and wrapped tight tonight. Buchanan's being picked up now. We'll see if he was in this, or if Maeve worked alone. But I'm damn sure she's the one who fired the gun. She's the one who lured Hopkins there. He had a weakness for young women. He'd never have felt threatened by her. Walked right in, alone, unarmed."

"If she sticks with this story about being Bobbie Bray, she could end up in a psychiatric facility instead of prison."

"A cage is a cage — the shape of it isn't my call."

At Central, Eve let Maeve stew a little while as she waited for Mira to be brought in and take a post in observation. So she took Buchanan first.

He was shaking when she went into interview room B, his face pale, his eyes glossy with distress.

"They said — they said you arrested my daughter. I don't understand. She'll need a lawyer. I want to get her a lawyer."

"She's an adult, Mr Buchanan. She'll request her own representation if she wants it."

"She won't be thinking straight. She'll be upset."

"Hasn't been thinking straight for a while, has she?"

"She's . . . she's delicate."

"Here." Peabody set a cup of water on the table for him. "Have a drink. Then you can help us help your daughter."

"She needs help," Eve added. "Do you know she claims to be Bobbie Bray?"

"Oh God. Oh God." He put his face in his hands. "It's my fault. It's all my fault."

"You are John Massey, grandson of Bobbie Bray and Radcliff Hopkins?"

"I got away from all that. I had to get away from it. It destroyed my mother. There was nothing I could do."

"So during the Urbans, you saw your chance. Planted your ID after an explosion. Mostly body parts. All that confusion. You walked away."

"I couldn't take all the killing. I couldn't go back home. I wanted peace. I just wanted some peace. I built a good life. Got married, had a child. When my wife died, I devoted myself to Maeve. She was the sweetest thing."

"Then you told her where she'd come from, who she'd come from."

He shook his head. "No. She told me. I don't know how she came to suspect, but she tracked down Rad Hopkins. She said it was business, and I wanted to believe her. But I was afraid it was more. Then one day she told me she'd been to Number Twelve, and she understood. She was going to take care of everything, but I never thought she meant . . . Is this ruining her life now, too? Is this ruining her life?"

"You knew she went back out the night Hopkins was killed," Eve said. "You knew what she'd done. She'd have told you. You covered for her. That makes you an accessory."

"No." Desperation was bright in his eyes as they darted around the room. "She was home all night. This is all a terrible mistake. She's upset and she's confused. That's all."

They let him sit, stepped out into the hall. "Impressions, Peabody?"

"I don't think he had an active part in the murder. But he knew — maybe put his head in the sand about it, but he knew. We can get him on accessory after the fact. He'll break once she has."

"Agreed. So let's go break her."

Maeve sat quietly. Her hair was smoothed again, her face was placid. "Lieutenant, Detective."

"Record on." Eve read the data into the recorder, recited the revised Miranda. "Do you understand your rights and obligations, Ms Buchanan?"

"Of course."

"So Maeve." Eve sat at the table across from her. "How long did you know Hopkins?"

A smirky little smile curved her lips. "Which one?"

"The one you shot nine times in Number Twelve."

"Oh, that Hopkins. I met him right after he bought the building. I read about it, and thought it was time we resolved some matters."

"What matters?"

"Him killing me."

"You don't look dead."

"He shot me so I couldn't leave him, so I wouldn't be someone else's money train. Then he covered it up. He covered me up. I've waited a long time to make him pay for it."

"So you sent him the message so he'd come to Number Twelve. Then you killed him."

"Yes, but we'd had a number of liaisons there before. We had to uncover my remains from that life."

"Bobbie Bray's remains."

"Yes. She's in me. I am Bobbie." She spoke calmly, as if they were once again sitting in the classy parlor in her brownstone. "I came back for justice. No one gave me any before."

"How did you know where the remains were?"

"Who'd know better? Do you know what he wanted to do? He wanted to bring in the media, to make another fortune off me. He had it all worked out. He'd bring the media in, let them put my poor bones on-screen, give interviews — at a hefty fee, of course. Using me again, like he always did. Not this time."

"You believed Rad Hopkins was Hop Hopkins reincarnated?" Peabody asked.

"Of course. It's obvious. Only this time I played him. Told him my father would pay and pay and pay for the letters I'd written. I told him where we had to open the wall. He didn't believe that part, but he wanted under my skirt."

She wrinkled her nose to show her mild distaste. "I could make him do what I wanted. We worked for hours cutting that brick. Then he believed."

"You took the hair clips and the gun."

"Later. We left them while he worked on his plan. While, basically, he dug his own grave. I cleaned them up. I really loved those hair clips. Oh, there were ammunition clips, too. I took them. I was there."

Her face changed, hardened, and her voice went raw, went throaty. "In me, in the building. So sad, so cold, so lost. Singing, singing every night. Why should I sing for him? Murdering bastard. I gave him a child, and he didn't want it."

"Did you?" Eve asked her.

"I was messed up. He got me hooked — the drugs, the life, the buzz, you know? Prime shit, always the prime shit for Hop. But I was going to get straight, give it up, go back for my kid. I was gonna — had my stuff packed up. I wrote and told my old lady, and I was walking on Hop. But he didn't want that. Big ticket, that's what I was. He never wanted the kid. Only me, only what I could bring in. Singing and singing."

"You sent Rad a message, to get him to Number Twelve."

"Sure. Public 'link, easy and quick. I told him to come, and when to come. He liked when I used Bobbie's voice — spliced from old recordings — in the messages I sent him. He thought it was sexy. Asshole. He stood there, grinning at me. I brought it, he said."

"What was it?"

"His watch. The watch he had on the night he shot me. The one I bought him when my album hit number one. He had it on his wrist and was grinning at me. I shot him, and I kept shooting him until the clip was empty. Then I pushed the murdering bastard over, and

I put the gun right against his head, right against it, and I shot him again. Like he did to me."

She sat back a little, smiled a little. "Now he can wander around in that damn place night after night after night. Let's see how he likes it."

# Epilogue

When Eve stepped out, rubbed her hands over her face, Mira slipped out of observation.

"Don't tell me," Eve began. "Crazy as a shithouse rat."

"That might not be my precise diagnosis, but I believe we'll find with testing that Maeve Buchanan is legally insane and in desperate need of treatment."

"As long as she gets it in a cage. Not a bit of remorse. Not a bit of fear. No hedging."

"She believes everything she did was justified, even necessary. My impression, at least from observing this initial interview, is she's telling you the truth exactly as she knows it. There's the history of mental illness on both sides of her family. This may very well be genetic. Then discovering who her great-grandmother was helped push her over some edge she may very well have been teetering on."

"How did she discover it?" Eve added. "There's a question. Father must have let something slip."

"Possibly. Haven't you ever simply known something? Or felt it? Of course, you have. And from what I'm told happened tonight, you had an encounter."

Frowning, Eve ran her fingers over her sore cheek. "I'm not going to stand here and say I was clocked by a ghost. I'm sure as hell not putting that in my report."

"Regardless, you may at the end of this discover the only reasonable way Maeve learned of her heritage was from Bobbie Bray herself. That she also learned of the location of the remains from the same source."

"That tips out of the reasonable."

"But not the plausible. And that learning these things snapped something inside her. Her way of coping was to make herself Bobbie. To believe she's the reincarnation of a woman who was killed before her full potential was realized. And who, if she'd lived — if she'd come back to claim her child — would have changed everything."

"Putting a lot of faith in a junkie," Eve commented. "And using, if you ask me, a woman who was used, exploited and murdered, to make your life a little more important."

Now she rubbed her eyes. "I'm going to get some coffee, then hit the father again. Thanks for coming down."

"It's been fascinating. I'd like to do the testing on her personally. If you've no objection."

"When I'm done, she's all yours."

Because her own AutoChef had the only real coffee in all of cop central, Eve detoured there first.

There he was, sitting at her desk, fiddling with his PPC.

"You should go home," Eve told Roarke. "I'm going to have an all-nighter on this."

"I will, but I wanted to see you first." He rose, touched his hand to her cheek. "Put something on that, will you?" Until she did, he put his lips there. "Do you have a confession?"

"She's singing — ha-ha. Chapter and verse. Mira says she's nuts, but that won't keep her out of lockup."

"Sad, really, that an obsession with one woman could cause so much grief, and for so long."

"Some of it ends tonight."

This time he laid his lips on hers. "Come back to me when you can."

"You can count on that one."

Alone, she sat. And alone she wrote up a report, and the paperwork that charged Radcliff C. Hopkins I with murder in the first degree in the unlawful death of Bobbie Bray. She filed it, then after a moment's thought, put in another form.

She requested the release of Bobbie Bray's remains to herself — if they weren't claimed by next of kin — so that she could arrange for their burial. Quietly.

"Somebody should do it," she stated aloud.

She got her coffee, rolled her aching shoulders. Then headed back to work.

In Number Twelve, there was silence in the dark. No one sang, or wept or laughed. No one walked there.

For the first time in eighty-five years, Number Twelve sat empty.

# ETERNITY IN DEATH

The Sun's rim dips; the stars rush out,
At one stride comes the dark.

SAMUEL TAYLOR COLERIDGE


Whence and what art thou, execrable
shape?

JOHN MILTON

# Prologue

Death was the end of the party. Worse than death, in Tiara's opinion, was what came before it. Age. The loss of youth, of beauty, of body and *celebrity* was the true horror. Who the hell wanted to screw an old, wrinkled woman? Who cared what some droopy bag of years wore to the hot new club, or what she didn't wear on the beach at the Côte d'Azur?

No-fucking-body, that's who.

So when he told her that death could be the beginning — the real beginning — she was fascinated. She was pumped. It made sense to her that immortality could be bought by those privileged enough to pay the price. All of her life everything she wanted, coveted or demanded had been bought, so eternal life wasn't any different, really, than her pied-à-terre in New York or her villa in France.

Immortality, unlike a penthouse or a pair of earrings, would never get boring.

She was twenty-three, and absolutely at her prime. Everything about her was tight and toned, which she assured herself of by examining her body in the mirror tube in her dressing room. She was perfect, she decided, giving her signature blonde mane a carefully studied, and meticulously practiced, toss.

Now, thanks to him, she would always be perfect.

She stepped out, leaving the double mirrored doors open so that she could watch herself dress. She'd chosen form-fitting, nearly transparent red, with a hem of peacock eyes that shimmered and winked with every movement. Chandelier drops swung at her ears, in the same vibrant tones of sapphire and emerald as the accents on the hem of the short, snug gown. She added her blue diamond pendant, and wide pave cuffs on both wrists.

Her sharply defined lips were dyed to match the dress, and they curved now with smug pride.

Later, she thought, after it was done, she'd change into something fun, something for dancing, for celebrating.

Her only regret was that the awakening had to be done in private rather than at the club. But her lover had assured her all that nasty business about being buried, then having to climb out of some disgusting coffin was just the invention of tacky books and bad vids. The reality was so much more civilized.

One hour after the ritual — which was so frigging sexy — she'd wake up in her own bed, eternally young, eternally strong, eternally beautiful.

Her new birthday would be April 18, 2060.

All it would cost was her soul. As if she cared about that.

She strolled out of the dressing room into the bedroom she'd just had redecorated in her new favorite shades of blues and greens. In his bed — canopied to match his mistress's — Tiara's teacup bulldog snored.

She wished she could awaken Biddy as she was about to be awakened. He was the only thing in the world she truly loved almost as much as herself. But she'd given her little sweetie pie the sleeping drug, just as she'd been told. It wouldn't do to have her doggie interrupt the ritual.

Following instructions, she disengaged all security on her private elevator and entrance, then lit the thirteen white candles she'd been told to set around the room she'd chosen for the awakening.

When it was done, she poured the bottle of potion he'd given her into a crystal wineglass. She drank it all, every drop. Nearly time, she thought, as she carefully arranged herself on the bed. He'd slip in quietly, find her. Take her.

Already she felt hot and jittery with need.

He'd make her scream, he'd make her come. And when she was screaming, when she was coming, he would give her that final, ultimate kiss.

Tiara traced her fingers over her throat, already feeling the bite.

She'd die, she thought, running her hands over her breasts and belly in anticipation of him. Wasn't that wild? She'd die, then she'd awaken. And she'd live forever.

# CHAPTER
## ONE

The room smelled of candle wax and death. In their fat, jewel-toned holders, the candles had pooled into dripping puddles. The body lay in a lake-sized bed canopied with silk, mounded with a multitude of pillows, and stained with blood.

She was young, blonde, with a bright red dress rucked up to her waist. Her eyes, a crystal green, were open and staring.

As she studied the body of Tiara Kent, Lieutenant Eve Dallas wondered if the dead blonde had looked into her killer's eyes as she died.

She'd known him, in any case, almost certainly she'd known him. There was no sign of forced entry, and in fact, the security system had been shut down from the inside, by the victim. There was no sign of struggle. And though Eve was certain they'd find the victim had engaged in sexual intercourse, she didn't believe it would prove to be rape.

She hadn't fought him, Eve thought as she bent over the body. Even when he'd drained the blood out of her, she hadn't fought him.

"Two puncture wounds, left side of the throat," Eve stated for the record. "The only visible injury." She lifted one of Tiara's hands, examined the perfectly shaped, fussily painted nails. "Bag the hands," she told her partner. "Maybe she scratched him."

"Not as much blood as you'd think there should be." Detective Peabody cleared her throat. "Not nearly enough. You know what they look like, on her neck there? Bite marks. Like, ah, fangs."

Eve spared Peabody a glance. "You think that ugly little dog the maid's got in the kitchen bit her on the neck?"

"No." Peabody angled her head, leaned down with her dark eyes wide and bright. "Come on, Dallas, you *know* what it looks like."

"It looks like a DB. It looks like the vic had a date that went over the top. There's going to be illegals in her system, something that dulled her down or hyped her up enough for her killer to jab something into her throat, or, yeah, sink his teeth into it if he had the incisors filed to points or was wearing an appliance. Then he bled her out, and she lay there and let him."

"I'm just saying it looks like your classic vampire bite."

"We'll put out an APB on Dracula. Meanwhile, let's find out if she was — just possibly — seeing someone with a heartbeat."

"Just saying," Peabody repeated, this time in a mumble.

Eve did another scan of the bedroom before stepping out and into the enormous dressing room area.

Bigger than a lot of apartments, she mused, and outfitted with a security screen, entertainment screen,

**128**

full round of mirrors. The closet itself was a small department store, ruthlessly organized into categories.

For a moment, Eve stood with her hands on her hips and simply stared. One person, she thought, with enough clothes to outfit the Upper West Side, and more than enough shoes to shod every man, woman, and child in that sector. Even Roarke — and Eve knew her husband's wardrobe was awesome — didn't rate this high on the clothes-hog scale.

Then she just shook her head and focused on the job at hand.

Dressed for him, Eve thought. Slutty dress, fuck-me heels. So where was the jewelry? If a woman was going to deck herself out for a booty call, down to shoes, wouldn't she drape on some glitters?

If she had, her killer had helped himself there.

She studied the drawers, the cabinets that ran below the rungs and carousels and protective domes. All locked, she noted, all passcoded, which meant valuables housed inside. There was no sign that she could see of any attempt to break in.

There were plenty of expensive bits and pieces sitting around in the penthouse: statuary, paintings, electronics. She'd seen nothing on her once-over of both levels that indicated anything had been disturbed.

If he was a thief, he was a lazy one, or a very picky one.

She stood for a moment, evaluating. Eve was a tall woman, slim in boots and trousers, with a short leather jacket over a white shirt. Her hair was short and brown, chopped around a lean face dominated by deep brown eyes. The eyes, as they studied, were all cop.

She didn't turn at Peabody's low whistle behind her. "Wow! This is like something out of a vid. I think she had all the clothes in all the land. And the *shoes*. Oooh, the shoes."

"A few hundred pair of shoes," Eve commented. "And she had the requisite two feet. People are screwy. Take head of building security, see if he's got any knowledge or documentation of who she's been seeing or entertaining in the last few weeks. I'll take the maid."

She moved through the apartment, down a level. The place was full of cops and crime-scene techs, of noise, of equipment. The busy business of murder.

In what she was told was the breakfast room, she found the maid with her red-rimmed eyes, clutching the small, ugly dog. Eve eyed the dog warily, then gestured for the uniforms to step out of the room.

"Ms Cruz?"

At the mention of her name, the woman burst into fresh sobs. This time Eve and the dog exchanged looks of mild annoyance.

Eve sat so she and the maid were on the same level, then said, firmly, "Stop it."

Obviously used to following orders, the maid instantly snuffled back the sobs. "I'm so upset," she told Eve. "Miss Tiara, poor Miss Tiara."

"Yes, I'm very sorry. You've worked for her for a while?"

"Five years."

"I know this is hard, but I need you to answer some questions now. To help me find who did this to Miss Tiara."

"Yes." The maid pressed a hand to her heart. "Anything. Anything."

"You have keys and passcodes to the apartment?"

"Oh, yes. I come in every day to do for Miss Tiara when she's in residence. And three times a week when she's away."

"Who else has access to the apartment?"

"No one. Well, maybe Miss Daffy. I'm not sure."

"Miss Daffy."

"Miss Tiara's friend, Daffodil Wheats. Her very best friend, except when they're fighting, then Miss Caramel is her best friend."

"Are you putting me on with these names?"

The maid blinked her swollen, bloodshot eyes. "No, ma'am."

"Lieutenant," Eve corrected. "All right, this Daffodil and Caramel were friends of Miss Kent's. What about men? What men was she seeing?"

"She saw a lot of men. She was so beautiful, so young, and so vibrant that —"

"Intimately, Ms Cruz," Eve interrupted to stop both the eulogy and the fresh tears. "And most recently."

"Please call me Estella. She enjoyed men. She was young and vibrant, as I said. I don't know them all — some were just a moment, others longer. But in the past week or two, I think there was just one."

"Who would that be?"

131

"I don't know. I never saw him. But I could tell she was in love again — she laughed more, and danced around the apartment, and . . ." Estella seemed to struggle for a moment with her own code of discretion.

"Everything you tell me may help in the investigation," Eve prompted.

"Yes. Well . . . when you take care of someone, you know when they've had a . . . an intimacy. She had a lover in her bed every night for a week or more."

"But you never saw him."

"Never. I come at eight every morning, and leave at six, unless she needs me to stay longer. He was never here when I was here."

"Was it her habit to turn off her security system from in-house?"

"Never, never." Dry-eyed now, Estella shook her head decisively from side to side. "It was never to be disengaged. I don't understand why she would have done that. I saw it was off when I came in this morning. I thought there must be a glitch in the system, and Miss Tiara would be angry. I called downstairs to report it even before I went up to the bedroom."

"All right. You came in at eight, noted the security was off, reported it, then went upstairs. Is that your usual routine, to come in, go up to her bedroom?"

"Yes, to get Biddy." Estella bent her head to nuzzle the dog. "To take him for his morning walk, then to feed him. Miss Tiara usually sleeps until about eleven."

Estella's brow creased. "Later these last days, since — the new lover. Sometimes she didn't come downstairs until into the afternoon, and she ordered all the windows draped when she did. She said she only wanted the night. It worried me because she looked so pale, and wouldn't eat. But I thought, well, she's in love, that's all."

After a long, long sigh, Estella continued. "Then this morning, Biddy wasn't waiting by the bedroom door. He always waits there for me in the morning. I went in, very quietly. He was coming to the door, but he wasn't walking right."

Eve frowned at the dog. "What do you mean?"

"It was . . . I thought: Biddy looks drunk, and I had to hold back a laugh because he looked so funny. I went in more, and I smelled . . . it was the candles at first. I could smell the candles, so I thought she'd had her lover in the night. But then there was another smell, a hard smell. It was the blood, I think," she said as her eyes welled again. "It must have been the blood and . . . her, I smelled her, and when I looked over at the bed, I saw her there. I saw my poor little girl there."

"Did you touch anything, Estella? Anything in the room?"

"No, no. Yes. Biddy. I grabbed Biddy. I don't know why exactly, I just grabbed little Biddy and I ran out. She was dead — the blood, her face, her eyes, everything. She couldn't be anything but dead. I ran out screaming, and I called security. Mr Tripps came right up. Right away, and he went upstairs. He was only a minute, then he came down to contact the police."

"Could you tell if anything's missing?"

"I know her things. I didn't notice . . ." Distressed again, she glanced around the room. "I didn't look."

"I'm going to have you look through her jewelry first. You know her jewelry?"

"I do. Every piece. I clean it for Miss Tiara because she doesn't trust —"

"Okay. We'll start there."

She sent Estella to the dressing area with two cops and a recorder. She was scribbling a few notes, adding time lines when Peabody tracked her down.

"Tripps reports that the maid contacted Security at eight-oh-two to report the system was down. She contacted them again at eight-oh-nine, hysterical. He came up personally, went upstairs, verified the death, contacted the police. Times jibe."

"Yeah, they do. What did he say about the system being down?"

"He said — and documented — that Kent told him she would be shutting it down internally near midnight, and would re-engage it when she wanted. He advised against, she told him to mind his own. She did the same every night for the last eight days, though the time of shutdown varied. She'd re-engage before dawn."

Thoughtfully, Eve tapped her fingers on her own notes. "So the boyfriend didn't want to be on the security tapes. Got her to shut it down, came in her private entrance, left the same way. She must've been monumentally stupid."

"Well, she wasn't known for her brains."

Eve slanted Peabody a look. If it was gossip or popular culture, Peabody usually had her finger on the pulse. "What was she known for?"

"Clubbing, shuttle-hopping, shopping, scandals. The usual, I guess, for a fourth-generation — I think it's fourth — megarich kid. She got engaged a lot, broke up a lot — usually publicly and with a lot of passion. Went to premieres, shuttled off to wherever the current hot spot might be. Hobbed and nobbed. Usually something on her in the tabs or one of the gossip or society channels every day."

"Who was she running with these days, and why did I feel I had to interview the maid about her lifestyle when I've got you?"

"Well, she's tight with Daffy Wheats, and Caramel Lipton, recently disengaged to Roman Gramaldi, of Zurich. But she hangs with the sparkles of the young, rich, and looking-for-trouble club."

"Trouble she found," Eve commented, then glanced up when Estella came rushing in.

"Her pendant, her blue diamond pendant, and the cuffs, her peacock earrings. Gone, all gone." Her voice pitched up sharply enough to cut glass. "He robbed my poor little girl, robbed her and killed her."

Eve held up a finger to stop the tirade. "Do you have photo documentation of the missing items?"

"Of course, of course. Insurance —"

"I'll need those. You get me the insurance information of whatever's missing. Go ahead." She waited until Estella hurried out again, smiled grimly. "That was a mistake. Sooner or later some big, fat blue diamond's going to show up. We'll get the details, then inform next of kin. After that, I want to have a chat with Daffy."

135

# CHAPTER
# TWO

As Tiara's mother was living with her fourth husband in Rome, and her father was currently vacationing on the Olympus Resort with his newest fiancée, notification was done via 'link.

Eve left the sweepers to finish processing the scene, and headed out with Peabody to interview Daffodil Wheats.

Another penthouse, Eve thought, another absurdly rich, young blonde. She badged and bullied her way past the doorman, past security, and finally past the housekeeper who might have been a clone of Estella Cruz. It turned out to be her sister.

The apartment was slightly smaller than Tiara's, a bit more tastefully furnished. They waited in a living area done in bold, vibrant colors while Martine Cruz went upstairs to wake her mistress and inform her the police wished to speak with her.

"What's the dish on this one, Peabody?"

"Um, third-generation rich, I think. Not as mega as the vic, but not worried about the grocery bill either. I think the fam made it big in textiles or something back in the day. Anyhow, she's another party girl and gossip channel regular."

"Who'd want to live like that?" Eve wondered.

"They do." Peabody gave a shrug. "You've got as much ready as they do, you can buy some privacy if you want it."

Eve thought back to the acres of mirrors and reflective surfaces at the crime scene. "The type who like to see themselves."

"Yeah, and unless Daffy and the vic were having one of their periodic fallings-out, they were pretty much joined at the hip. Played together, traveled together, and rumor has it shared some of the same men, maybe at the same time. Been tight since they were kids. Vic's father was married to Daffy's mother — or cohabbed, can't remember — for a couple of years."

"Small, incestuous little world."

Eve glanced up. Daffodil Wheats had a short, streaky crop of blonde hair, sleepy blue eyes, and a sulky mouth. She wore a black silk robe that hit her midthigh and gaped open at the breasts so the full white mounds of them played peek-a-boo as she walked down the swirl of silver steps.

"What's the deal?" she said in a blurry voice, then plopped down on the bright red sofa and yawned.

"Daffodil Wheats?" Eve demanded.

"Yeah, yeah. God, it's barely dawn. Martine! I'm desperado for that mocha! I was out 'til four," she explained with a long, feline stretch. "I didn't do anything illegal, so what's what with the badges?"

"You know Tiara Kent?"

"Hell, what's Tee done now?" She slumped, obviously already bored. "Look, I'll bail her, even if she has been a bitch lately. But I have to have my fix first. Mocha, mocha, mocha!" she shouted like an Arena Ball cheer.

"I'm sorry to tell you that Tiara Kent is dead."

The sleepy eyes narrowed a little, then rolled dramatically. "Oh, get off. You tell Princess Bitch that dragging me out of bed to lay it on didn't get a chuckle. Thank God! Thanks, Martine. Life saved." She made kissy noises at the maid as she grabbed the tall white cup of steaming liquid.

"Listen up, *Daffy*." Eve's tone had the blue eyes blinking in surprise. "Your pal was murdered last night, in her bed. So you're going to want to straighten your ass up — and cover your tits, for God's sake — or we're going to take the rest of this downtown."

"That's not funny." Slowly now, Daffy lowered the cup. "That's seriously un." The hand holding the cup shook as Daffy reached out for Martine with the other. "Martine, call Estella. Call her right now and have her put Tiara on the 'link."

"She can't come to the 'link." Peabody spoke now, more gently. "Ms Kent was killed last night in her apartment."

"My sister," Martine said even as she gripped Daffy's hand.

"Your sister's fine," Peabody told her. "You can go ahead and contact her."

"Miss Daffy."

"Go on," Daffy said stiffly, and the bored young party girl was gone. In her place was a stunned young woman clutching her robe together at her throat with a

**138**

trembling hand. "Go on, go on. This isn't a joke, this isn't Tee taking a slap at me? She's dead?"

"Yes."

"But . . . I don't see how that can be. She's only twenty-three. You're not supposed to be dead at twenty-three, and we're fighting. We can't be fighting when she's dead. How . . . Killed? Did you say somebody killed Tee?"

Now Eve sat, choosing the glossy white table in front of the sofa so she and Daffy were on a level. "She's been seeing someone recently."

"What? Yeah. But . . ." Daffy looked around blankly. "What?"

Reaching out, Eve took the cup of mocha from Daffy's limp fingers, set it aside. "Do you know the name of the man she's been seeing recently?"

"I . . . She called him her prince. Lots of times she had names for her men. This one was Prince. Dark Prince, sometimes." Daffy pressed her hands to her eyes, then dragged them up over her face, through her hair. "She's only been into him for a week or so. Maybe two. I can't think." She put her hand to her head, rubbed her temple as if she couldn't keep her fingers still. "I can't think."

"Can you describe him?"

"I never met him. I was supposed to, but I didn't. We've been fighting," she repeated as tears spilled down her cheeks.

"Tell me what you know about him."

"Did he hurt her?" Her voice broke on the question as the tears started to gush. "Did he kill Tee?"

"We're going to want to talk to him. Tell me what you know about him."

"She . . . she met him at some underground club. I was supposed to go, but I got hung up, and I forgot. I was supposed to meet her there."

"Where?" Eve prompted.

"Um . . . a cult club, underground, near Times Square, I think. I can't remember. There are so many." When Peabody offered tissues, Daffy sent her a pathetically grateful look. "Thanks. Thanks. She — Tee, she tagged me about eleven when I didn't show, and we got into it because I'd forgotten, and this guy I hooked up with and I decided to zip down to South Beach for the night. I was already down there when she tagged me."

On a long breath, she bent forward to retrieve the cup of mocha, and now sipped slowly. "Okay. Okay." She breathed in and out. "It was my screwup, about the club, so I mea culpa'd the next day. She was all about this guy, this Prince. But she looked out of it, so I knew she'd been using."

Daffy pressed her lips together. "I'm clean, and I've got to stay clean. My father still holds some of the purse strings on me, you know? If I get in any trouble like that again, he said he'd cut me off. He means it, so . . . Shit, you're cops, I'm not going to impress you, so the straight deal is this: Besides the edict from my dad, I've had enough of chems."

"But Tiara hadn't," Eve said.

"Tee's always going to go over the top, it's just her way. Always going to push the limits, then look for the

**140**

next big thing." As Daffy mopped tears, she managed a wan smile. "But she knows I've got to stay clean. She'd been using, and she'd sworn off six months ago, like a solidarity deal? We took an oath, so I was pissed."

"What was she on?" Eve asked.

"I don't know, but she was strung. We scratched at each other about that, but it was mostly her telling me how I had to go with her to this club, meet this guy and his friends. She said he was complete, the absolute. That they'd banged all night, and it was the best she'd ever had. She nagged me brainless about it until I said I'd go."

Shaking her head, Daffy drank again. "Then later I started thinking how even if I didn't use, she would, and I'd get busted. So I tagged her back and told her I wasn't going, and why didn't we hook up with this guy somewhere else. No go. His club or nowhere."

"His club?"

"Not like he owned it. Or maybe he does. She never said; I never asked. But she got stewed because I wouldn't go, and Carm's in New LA until next month, so she couldn't pull her instead of me."

Eve waited while Daffy brooded into the mocha she'd so desperately wanted. "Do you know if anyone else went with her to this club? Any of your other mutual friends?"

"I don't think so. I never heard any buzz about it, not from anyone but Tee. Anyway, we didn't talk for a couple days, then yesterday she came by here, earlier than this even. Like just after sunrise. She looked bottomed. Pale and glassy-eyed. Using again, and she hadn't been using before this run for that whole six months. She was still hyped, talking wild. Going to live forever, that's what she said. Laughing and busting around. She and her prince were going to live forever, and screw me for flipping her off. I tried to get her to stay, but she wouldn't, just told me I'd be sorry, I'd had my chance. Now he was only taking her."

"Taking her where?" Eve asked.

"I don't know. She wasn't making any sense. I'm telling you, she was over. I got pissy right back at her, and we yelled at each other, then she stormed out. And now she's dead."

"That's the last time you saw or spoke with her?"

"Yeah. Did he hurt her? I mean . . . you didn't say how she, she died. Did he hurt her?"

"I can't tell you that yet, I'm sorry."

"She's such a baby about pain." Daffy swiped the back of her hand over her cheek. "I hope he didn't hurt her. I should've gone to the club that night. If I'd gone to the club instead of South Beach, maybe . . . Is it my fault? I should've looked after her better. She got sucked into stuff so easy. Is it my fault?"

"No, it's not your fault."

"She was almost a year older, but I was the one who looked after her — mostly. I could pull her back from the edge when she went too far. But I didn't, you know? I just told her she was being an idiot or whatever. Only Tee would actually believe in vampires."

"Vampires?" Eve repeated as Peabody sucked in her breath.

142

"Yeah. The prince deal? The Dark Prince. Living forever. Get it?" Daffy gave a harsh laugh that choked on a sob. "She thought this guy was a frigging vampire, like for real, and he was going to make her one so she'd be immortal. That's what the club was — a wannabe vampire club. Bloodbath! I remember now. It's called Bloodbath. Who the hell wants to go to some club with a name like that?" She swiped at tears again. "Only Tee."

"Didn't I say vampire? I said vampire right off." Peabody gave a smug nod as they exited the building.

"And our vic's going to be deeply disappointed when she just stays dead. Track down this club. I'd love a little chat with the Dark Prince."

"It's not like I believe in the undead or anything." Peabody slid into the passenger seat. "But it wouldn't hurt, once we find this guy, to interview him during the day. In a room with good natural lighting."

"Sure. And requisition some garlic and some wooden stakes while you're at it."

"Really?"

"No." Eve swung out into traffic. "Reach down inside yourself, Peabody, and get a grip on reality, however slippery. Find the club. Right now we're going to visit somebody who knows all about what's dead."

Chief Medical Examiner Morris sent Eve an easy smile as he stood over the naked body of Tiara Kent. He wore a snappy suit the color of good claret with a matching tie thin as straw. His dark hair was intricately braided, and curled into a loop at the nape of his neck.

Eve often thought Morris's sharp fashion sense was wasted on his clientele.

"Running a bit behind today," he told them. "Sent off for tox as you'd flagged that. Shouldn't take long."

She glanced down at the body. Morris hadn't yet made his Y cut. "What can you tell me just from the visual?"

"Lieutenant, this woman is dead."

"Peabody, note that down. We've got a dead woman."

"With excellent breast work," Morris added. "And some very first-class sculpting, belly and butt."

"Jesus, she was twenty-three. Who needs sculpting and new tits at twenty-three?"

Peabody raised her hand, and got a bland look from Eve.

"You're not twenty-three."

"Okay, I've got a couple years on her, but if they're handing out butt sculpting, I'm first in line."

"You have a very nice butt, Detective," Morris assured her, and made Peabody beam.

"Aw, thanks."

"And now, back to our regularly scheduled program?" Eve suggested. "The dead woman on the slab."

"Tiara Kent, party princess. Live fast, die young." Morris tapped his comp screen to magnify the neck wounds. "These are the only injuries or insults to the body. The victim was exsanguinated through these two punctures in the carotid. No visible signs of physical restraint or struggle. Apparently, she lay there and let him suck her dry."

"Suck." Peabody drew a righteous breath through her nose. "See? Vampire bite."

Morris's smile spread to a grin. "Impossible not to have a little play with that, isn't it? The beautiful young blonde, seduced by the Prince of Darkness — or one of his minions — drained of her life's blood while in his thrall. Cue fog and shadows."

"Don't forget the creepy music," Eve added.

"Of course. Mostly, however, I suspect she was drugged to the eyeballs, and was punctured by an appliance during sex."

He lifted his eyebrows as he looked down at Tiara. "Of course, I could be wrong, and she'll pop up shortly after sundown and terrify the night staff."

"Let's go with number one," Eve decided. "If he actually bit her, appliance or not, there's going to be saliva. Same if he didn't use a cloak for sex. I bet even vampires have DNA."

"I'll send samples to the lab."

"Guy had her convinced he could give her eternity." Eve took one last look at Tiara Kent. "Now she gets a steel box in a cold room."

# CHAPTER
# THREE

"Got the club." Peabody studied the readout on her PPC as they drove toward Cop Central. "Daffy had it right about Times Square, it's under Broadway. Got the hours, too. Sunset to sunrise." Peabody tracked her eyes toward Eve's profile. "Vampire hours."

"Owner?"

"Eternity Corporation, no owner or manager listed in this data."

"Dig," Eve suggested.

"Digging. Are we going by the club now?"

"If the guy frequents the place, works in the place, or owns the place, he's not going to be there when the joint's closed. We'll go after dark."

"I knew you were going to say that. Aren't you just a little bit creeped? I mean, at the very least this guy slurps blood."

"Maybe he does, maybe he doesn't." Eve stopped at a light, and watched the throng bull, shuffle, and clip its way along the crosswalk. She saw a pair of transvestites in spangled skin-suits, a tourist approaching three hundred and fifty pounds in his baggy shorts — carrying a variety of cams and vids that had to weigh nearly what he did — a kid in a red cape and skullcap streaking through bodies on an airboard, and a mime.

Whatever weirdos existed, New York made them welcome. A self-proclaimed vampire would fit right in.

"She didn't leave a full pint on the sheets," Eve continued as the light changed. "I don't care how hungry some pseudovampire is, no way he's going to guzzle down more than eight pints of blood in a sitting."

"Right. Right. Well, then what . . ."

"He took it with him."

"I have to say eeuuw."

"Bottled it up, bagged it up. Maybe he sells it, maybe he stores it, maybe he takes a fucking bath in it. But he came prepped for it." She turned into the garage at Central. "So we work that. What's a guy do with several pints of human blood? Let's see if there's a call for it on the black market. And we have the list and description of the jewelry missing from the scene. We've got the club."

She pulled into her slot, climbed out. "We'll see what the sweepers got for us, see if the lab can pull DNA. We'll check like crimes, see if we got anything like this before."

Once inside the elevator, Eve leaned back. The car smelled like cop — coffee and sweat. "Somebody saw her with this guy. She hooked up with him at the club, and somebody saw them together. She goes for thrills, gets drawn in. Starts letting him into her place, fun and games. The way it looks, he could've killed her any time he wanted, robbed her freaking blind. But he waited, and he only took what she either had on or had out.

"He's picky, and he likes the ritual, likes the seduction."

Eve stepped off the car to switch to the glides before the elevator got crowded. "Go ahead and write up what we've got, keep looking for a name to go with the club. I'm going to try to get a session in with Mira, get a better idea of what we'll be dealing with when we take ourselves a Bloodbath."

"I'll bring the rubber ducky."

Eve peeled off in the bullpen, headed for her office. As she expected, her 'link was loaded with calls from the media. A paparazzi darling ends up dead, it's a ratings bonanza, she thought, and ruthlessly forwarded all of the calls to the media liaison.

She tried for Mira first and ran headfirst into Mira's admin — the guardian at the doctor's gate. "Okay, okay. Jesus. Just tell her I'd like five whenever she can spare it. Here, there, in adjoining stalls in the John. Just five."

Eve disconnected, got coffee from her AutoChef. She set up her murder board, wrote up her notes, studied the time line.

Walked right in, that's what he did. She practically showered his path with rose petals. More money than brains.

Did he mark her first, or was it just chance she walked into the club one night? A recognizable face that liked to dance on the wild side. Known more for her exploits than her smarts.

A pathetically easy mark.

But if it had been just for the score, why kill her at all, much less in the chosen method? Because the score was secondary, she decided. The killing was the prize.

Eve glanced toward her tiny window, into the light of a sunny spring day, and calculated the time until sundown.

Thinking of that, she winced, engaged her 'link again. She wasn't just a cop, she reminded herself, but a wife. There were rules in both jobs.

She tried Roarke's private line, intending to leave a voice mail telling him she'd be late, see you when, but he picked up on the first beep. And that face, the heat-in-the-belly sexuality of that face, filled her view screen.

Dark hair framed it. Eyes of wild Irish blue gave her heart just a quick flutter that even after two years of having them look at her, just that way, was a surprise. Those perfectly sculpted lips curved as he said, "Lieutenant," with the wisp of his homeland in the word.

"How come you're not busy buying Australia?"

"I'm just between buying continents at the moment. I believe Asia's up next. And how are you?"

"Okay. I know we had sort of a thing on for tonight —"

"Dinner, I believe it was, followed by naked poker."

"That was strip poker, as I recall."

"You'd be naked soon enough. But I'm thinking that competition's been postponed. You have Tiara Kent, I take it."

"Heard about her already?"

"Multimillionaire bad girl murdered in her luxury penthouse?" His eyebrows lifted. "Word travels. How did she die?"

"Vampire bite."

"That again?" he said and made her laugh.

"She was into some kind of vampire cult crap, and it came back to, well, bite her. I've got to check out this club where she likely met her killer. It doesn't open until sunset, so I'm going to run late."

"Almost as interesting as naked poker. I'll meet you at Central by six. Darling Eve," he continued before she could speak, "you can't expect me to pass up the opportunity to accompany my wife into the den of the undead."

She considered a moment. He'd be useful; he always was. And another pair of eyes, another set of reflexes would come in handy underground.

"Don't be late."

"I'll leave in plenty of time. Should I pick up some garlic and crosses on the way?"

"I think Peabody's on that. Later," she said, and clicked off.

While she was at her desk, she contacted the lab to give them a not-so-gentle push, then began to research vampire lore. She broke off when Peabody poked her head in.

"Did you know there are dozens of websites on vampirism, and any number of them have instructions on how to drink from a victim?"

Peabody cocked her head. "This surprises you because?"

"I know I say people suck, but I didn't mean it literally. And it's not just kids in their I'm-so-bored twenties into this."

"I've got a couple of names we might want to look at, but meanwhile, Tiara Kent's mother just came in. I had one of the uniforms take her to the lounge."

"Okay, I'll take her, you keep digging." Eve pushed back from her desk. "Roarke's going to tag along tonight."

"Yeah?" Relief showed on Peabody's face before she controlled it. "It doesn't hurt to have more of us when we head down."

"He's an observer," Eve reminded her. "I'm waiting for a callback from Mira. That comes through, tag me."

Eve made Iris Francine the minute she stepped into the lounge with its lines of vending machines and little tables, and chairs designed to numb the ass after a five-minute sit-down.

Her daughter had favored her, taking the blonde hair, the green eyes, the delicate bone structure from her mother.

Iris sat with her hand clutched by a man Eve imagined was husband number four, Georgio Francine. Younger than his wife by a few years, Eve judged, and dark and sultry where she was light and elegant.

But they sat like a unit — she recognized that. Like two parts of a whole.

"Ms Francine, I'm Lieutenant Dallas."

151

Iris's eyes looked exhausted as they lifted to Eve's, a combination Eve also recognized as grief, guilt, and simple fatigue.

"You're the one in charge of . . . in charge of what happened to Tiara."

"That's right." Eve pulled up a chair. "I'm very sorry for your loss."

"Thank you. Will I able to see her?"

"I'll arrange that for you."

"Can you tell me how she . . . what happened to her?" Iris's breath hitched, and she took two slow ones to smooth it out. "They won't tell me anything really. It's worse not knowing."

"She was killed last night, in her apartment. We believe she knew her killer, and let him in herself. Some pieces of her jewelry are missing."

"Was she raped?"

They would always ask, Eve knew. For a daughter, they would always ask, and with their eyes pleading for the answer to be no. "She'd had sexual relations, but we don't believe there was rape."

"An accident?" There was another plea in Iris's voice now, as if death wouldn't be as horrible somehow if it were accidental. "Something that got out of hand?"

"No, I'm sorry. We don't believe it was an accident. What do you know about your daughter's activities recently, her companions? The men in her life?"

"Next to nothing." Iris closed her eyes. "We didn't communicate much, or often. I wasn't a good mother."

"*Cara.*"

"I wasn't." She shook her head at her husband's quiet protest. "I was only twenty when she was born, and I wasn't a good mother. I wasn't a good anything." The words were bitter with regret. "It was all parties and fun and where can we go next. When Tiara's father had an affair, I had one to pay him back. And on and on, until we loathed each other and used her as a weapon."

She turned her shimmering eyes to her husband as he lifted their joined hands, pressed his lips to her fingers. "Long ago," he said softly. "That was long ago."

"She never forgave me. Why should she? When we divorced, Tee's father and I, I married again like that." Iris snapped her fingers. "Just to show him he didn't matter. I paid for that mistake six months later, but I didn't learn. When I finally grew up, it was too late. She preferred her father, who'd let her do whatever she liked, with whomever she liked."

"You made mistakes," Georgio told her. "You tried to fix them."

"Not hard enough, not soon enough. We have an eight-year-old daughter," she told Eve. "I'm a good mother to her. But I lost Tiara long ago. Now I can never get her back. The last time we spoke, more than a month ago, we argued. I can never get that back either."

"What did you argue about?"

"Her lifestyle, primarily. I hated that she was wasting herself the way I did. She was pushing, pushing the boundaries more all the time. Her father's engaged again, and this one's younger than Tee. It enraged her, had her obsessing about getting older, losing her looks.

**153**

Can you imagine, worried about such things at twenty-three?"

"No." Eve thought of the mirrors again, the clothes, the body work Tiara had done. Obviously, this was a young woman who obsessed about anything that had to do with herself. "Did she have any particular interest in the occult?"

"The occult? I can't say. She went through a period several years ago where she paid psychics great gobs of money. She dabbled in Wicca when she was a teenager — so many girls do — but she said there were too many rules. She was always looking for the easy way, for some magic potion to make everything perfect. Will you find who killed her?"

"I'll find him."

Even as Eve made arrangements to have the Francines transported to the morgue, she saw Mira come in. After an acknowledging nod, Mira wandered to a vending machine.

She'd cut her hair again, Eve noted, so it was short and springy at the nape of her neck, and she'd done something to that soft sable color so that little wisps of it around her face were a paler tone. She sat, trim and pretty in her blue-bonnet-colored suit, with two tubes of Diet Pepsi.

"Iris Francine," Mira stated when Eve came over. "I recognized her. Her face was everywhere a generation ago. I always thought her daughter was hell-bent on outdoing her mother's youthful exploits. It seems she succeeded in the hardest possible way."

154

"Yeah, dying will get you considerable face time, for a while."

"Quite a while, I'll wager in this case. Vampirism. I had a meeting one level up," Mira explained, "and thought to catch you in your office. Peabody gave me the basics. Murder by vampire proponents is very rare. For the most part, it's the danger, the thrill, the eroticism that draws people — primarily young people. There is a condition —"

"Renfield Syndrome. I've been reading up. What I'm getting from the people who knew the vic was a predilection to walk the edge, a desperation for fame, attention, a serious need to be and stay young and beautiful. She'd already had bodywork. And you have to add in sheer stupidity. I get her. She's not unusual, she just had more money than most so she could indulge her every idiocy."

Eve paused as she broke the seal on the Pepsi tube. "It's him. The method of killing was very specific, planned out, and there was no attempt to disguise it. He took jewelry, but that was more of the moment than motive. He went there to do exactly what he did, in exactly the way he did it."

"The compulsion may be his," Mira considered. "A craving for the taste of blood, one that escalated to the need to drain his victim. Have you gotten the autopsy results as yet?"

"No."

"I wonder if they'll find she drank blood as well. If so, you may be dealing with a killer who believes he's a vampire, and who sought to turn her into one by taking her blood and sharing his own with her."

"And if at first you don't succeed?"

"Yes." Mira's eyes, a softer blue than her suit, met Eve's. "He may very well try again. The rush, the power — particularly when coupled with sex and drugs — would be a strong pull. And she made it so easy for him, even profitable."

"How could he resist?"

"And why should he?" Mira concurred. "He was able to enter her highly secured building undetected. More power, and again cementing the illusion of a supernatural being. She gave herself to him, through sex, through blood, through death. Held in thrall — whether by his will or chemicals — another element. He removed her blood from the scene. A souvenir perhaps, a trophy, or yet another element of his power. His need for blood, and his ability to take it. You believe she was drugged?"

"I haven't had that confirmed, but yeah. Her closest pal states she'd been using, and heavily, the last week or so."

"If he drank any of her blood, he'd have shared the drug." Seeing Eve had already considered that, Mira nodded. "More power, or the illusion of it. From what you know, they'd only met a week or two earlier. It wasn't eternal love, which is one way of romanticizing vampirism."

"I don't get that." Interrupting, Eve gestured with her drink. "The romantic part."

Mira's lips curved. "Because you're a pragmatic soul. But for some, for many, the idea of eternity, that seeking a mate throughout it, coupled with the living by night, the lack of human boundaries is extremely romantic."

"Takes all kinds."

"It does. However, the way he left the body wasn't romantic, or even respectful. It was careless, cold. Whether or not he believes he could sire a vampire through her, she was no more than a vessel to him, a means to an end.

"He'll be young," Mira continued. "No more than forty. Most likely attractive in appearance and in good health. Who would want eternal life if they were homely and physically disadvantaged?"

"This vic wouldn't have gone for anyone who wasn't pretty anyway. Too vain. Her place was loaded with mirrors."

"Hmm. I wonder how she resigned herself to the lore that she'd have no reflection as a vampire."

"Could be she only bought what she wanted to buy."

"Perhaps. He'll be precise, erudite, clever. Sensual. He may be bisexual, or believe himself to be as in lore, vampires will bed and bite either sex. He will, at least for the moment, feel invulnerable. And that will make him very dangerous."

Eve drank some of her soft drink, smiled. "Knowing I'm mortal makes me very dangerous."

# CHAPTER
# FOUR

Eve grabbed the tox report the second it came through. Then she stared at the results. She engaged her interoffice 'link, said only, "Peabody," then went back to studying the lab's findings.

"Yo," Peabody said a moment later at Eve's office doorway.

"Tox report. Take a look." Eve passed her a printout while she continued to read her computer screen.

"Holy crap. It's not what she took," Peabody decided, "it's more what didn't she take."

"Hallucinogens, date-rape drugs, sexual enhancers, paralytic, human blood, tranq, all mixed in wine. Hell of a cocktail."

"I've never seen anything like this." Peabody glanced over the printout. "You?"

"Not with so many variables and with this potency. It's new to me, but let's run it by Illegals and see if it's new to them. According to the results, and the time line, she downed this herself, before she disengaged the alarm, or just after. Maybe she knew what was in it, maybe she didn't. But she drank it down, on her own."

"Hard to say, seeing she's dead, but she pretty much wins the stupid prize."

"All-time champ." Eve paused as her machine signalled another incoming. "And we may have a runner-up. We've got DNA." She scanned the data quickly. "Semen, saliva, and the blood she ingested. All the same donor."

"Pretty damn careless of him," Peabody commented.

"Yeah." Eve frowned at the screen. "It is, isn't it?"

"Another conclusion is he just didn't care — being a vampire." Peabody shrugged as Eve glanced back at her. "He doesn't care if we match his DNA because he'll just, I don't know, turn into a bat and fly off, or poof into smoke. Whatever."

"Right. A whole new scope on going into the wind."

"I'm not saying it's what I think, but maybe what he thinks."

"We'll be sure to ask him when we find him. Meanwhile, go ahead and run the cocktail by Illegals. I'll do a standard search for the DNA match. Maybe he's in the system."

But she didn't think so. He wasn't careless, Eve thought. He was fucking arrogant. It didn't surprise her when her search turned up negative.

"Lieutenant."

She glanced over, experienced that quick heart punch when her eyes met Roarke's. He was dressed in the dark suit he'd put on in their bedroom that morning, one of the countless he owned tailored to fit his long, rangy frame.

"Right on time," she said.

"We aim to please." He stepped in, eased a hip onto the corner of her desk. "How goes the vampire hunting?"

"I don't think we'll have to call in Van Helsing." When he lifted his brows and grinned, she shrugged. "I do my research. Plus I've sat through some of those old vids you like so much."

"And so armed, we'll venture into the den of the children of the night. Never a dull moment," he added and flicked his fingers at the choppy ends of her hair. "Your case is all over the media."

"Yeah. Bound to be."

"I noticed the primary hasn't given a statement."

"I'm not going to play the game on this one, or give this asshole the satisfaction. She drugged her own brains out prior — mix of Zeus, Erotica, Whore, Rabbit, Stunner, Bliss, Boost, along with a few other goodies, including her killer's blood."

"There's an ugly recipe."

"And my money says he provided the brew, pushed on her vanity and stupid buttons, got his rocks off, then drained her like a faulty motor."

"For what purpose?" Roarke wondered.

"Best I can tell, he wound her up because he could. And he killed her because he could. He'll want to do it again, real soon."

"Foolish of him, don't you think, to have chosen such a high-profile victim?"

She'd considered that, and had to appreciate being married to a man who could think like a cop. "Yeah, smarter, safer to bite a vagrant off the street. But this was more fun, more exciting. Why snack on street whores or side-walk sleepers, the nobodies, when you can gorge yourself on the prime? Plus, it was profitable. A street level LC isn't going to be sporting blue diamonds. He's stoked, believe it, watching all the media coverage."

**160**

"Unless he's spent the day napping in his coffin."

"Ha, ha." She pushed up, instinctively brushed a hand over the weapon at her side. "Almost sundown. Let's go clubbing."

Peabody was lying in wait, along with her cohab, E-Division Detective McNab. He wasn't just a fashion plate, but an entire place setting, and was decked out in pants of neon blue that appeared to be made up almost entirely of pockets. He'd matched it with a bright green jacket with streaks of yellow jagged across it and some sort of skinny tank that melded all the colors of the spectrum in a kind of eye-searing cloudburst.

"I thought we could use another pair of eyes," Peabody began even as Eve's eyes narrowed. "You know, strength in numbers."

"I did a rotation in Illegals when I was still in uniform." McNab grinned out of his pretty, narrow face. "And when I worked Vice, we ran into all kinds of freaky shit."

"You don't want to miss a chance to cruise a vampire club."

He smile turned winsome. "Who would?"

She could use him, Eve thought, but she gave him the hard-eye first, just for form. "This isn't a damn double date."

"No, sir." So he waited until Eve turned her back to walk to the elevator before hooking pinkies with Peabody.

"Illegals hasn't worked the combo," Peabody began once they'd shoehorned into the elevator. "They don't even have Bloodbath on their list of watch points. But they have worked a combination of Erotica, Bliss, Rabbit, with traces of blood — usually animal blood —

in cases of vampire fetishism. They call it Vamp, and the use generally skews young. They haven't had any homicides as a result of."

"Our guy upped the stakes, considerably. Have to wonder why the club hasn't made their list."

"It's new," Peabody told her. "Way underground. Hadn't hit their radar until I contacted them regarding our investigation."

"Underground clubs pop up faster than weeds," McNab put in. "Live or die on word of mouth. Since it's more than urban legend that people tend to go down and not come back up, they don't get heavy tourist traffic."

"Tiara Kent found out about it somewhere." Eve strode off the elevator and into the garage.

"Crowd she runs with." Peabody jerked a shoulder. "New place with a jagged edge? It would be right up her alley."

"And in less than two weeks from the first time she goes down, she's guzzling a new, exciting illegals cocktail, and dies from a neck wound." Eve slid behind the wheel of her vehicle. "That's fast work, smooth work when you consider the security in her building never made him." She glanced over at Roarke. "How much would a few pints of human blood net on the black market?"

"A few hundred."

"What about famous human blood?"

"Ah." He nodded as she drove out of the garage. "Yes, that might drive up the price to the right buyer. Are you thinking she was specifically targeted?"

"It's an angle. She's known, and she's known to take risks, to slut around, to live wild. Her best friend hadn't heard of the club before Kent clued her in. So maybe the idea or an invitation got passed straight onto the vic. In any case, she hooked up with her killer there, so someone saw them together. Someone knows him."

"You know," McNab speculated, "if you factor out the blood-sucking, soulless demon angle, this should be a slam dunk."

"Good thing none of us believe in blood-sucking, soulless demons." But Peabody's hand crept over and found McNab's.

Eve caught the gesture in the rearview, just as she caught the way the fingers of Peabody's free hand snuck between the buttons of her shirt to close over something.

"Peabody, are you wearing a cross?"

"What? Me?" The hand dropped like a stone into her lap. Her cheeks went pink as she cleared her throat. "It just happened that I know Mariella in Records, who just happened to have one, and I happened to borrow it. Just for backup."

"I see. And would you also be carrying a pointy stick?"

"Not unless you mean McNab."

McNab smiled easily as Eve stopped at a light, turned around in her seat. "Repeat after me: Vampires do not exist."

"Vampires do not exist," Peabody recited.

With a nod, Eve turned back, then narrowed her eyes at Roarke. "What's that look on your face?"

"Speculation. Most legends, after all, have some basis in fact. From Vlad the Impaler to Dracula of lore. It's interesting, don't you think?"

"It's interesting that I'm in this vehicle with a trio of lamebrains."

"Lamebrained to some," Roarke replied equably, "open-minded to others."

"Huh. Maybe we should stop off at a market on the way, pick up a few pounds of garlic, just to ease those open minds."

"Really?" Peabody said from the back, then hunched her shoulders as Eve sent her a stony stare in the rearview mirror. "That means no," Peabody muttered to McNab.

"I translated already."

Eve had to settle for a second-level street slot five blocks from the underground entrance. The sun had set, and the balmy April day had gone to chill with a wind that had risen up to kick through the urban canyons.

They moved through the packs of pedestrians — heading home, heading to dinner, heading to entertainment. At the mouth of the underground entrance, Eve paused.

"Stick together through the tunnels," she ordered. "We can work in pairs once we get to the club, but even then, let's keep visual contact at all times."

She didn't believe in the demons of lore, but she knew the human variety existed. And many of them lived, played, or worked in the bowels of the city.

They moved down, out of the noise, out of the wind, into the dank dimness of the tunnels. The clubs and haunts and dives that existed there catered to a clientele that would make most convicted felons sprint in the opposite direction.

Offerings underground included sex clubs that specialized in S&M, in torture dealt out for a fee by human, droid, or machine, or any miserable combination thereof. In the bars, the drinks were next to lethal and a man's life was worth less than the price of a shot. The violent and the mad might wander there, sliding off into the shadows to do what could only be done in the dark, where blood and death bloomed like fetid mushrooms.

She could hear weeping, raw and wild, echoing down one of the tunnels, and laughter that was somehow worse. She saw one of the lost addicts, pale as a ghost, huddled on the filthy floor, panting, pushing a syringe against his arm, giving himself a fix of what would eventually kill him.

She turned away from it, passed a sex club where the lights were hard and red and reminded her of the room in Dallas where she'd killed her father.

It was cold underground, as it had been cold in that room. The kind of cold that sank its teeth into the bone like an animal.

She heard something scuttling to the left, and saw the gleam of eyes. She stared into them until they blinked, and they vanished.

"I should've given you my clutch piece," she said under her breath to Roarke.

"Not to worry. I have my own."

She spared him a glance. He looked, she realized, every bit as deadly as anything that roamed the tunnels. "Try not to use it."

They turned down an angle beyond a vid parlor where someone screamed in a hideous combination of pain and delight.

She smelled piss and vomit as they descended the next level. When a man with bulging muscles stepped out of the dark, turned the knife he held into the slant of light so it gleamed, Eve simply drew her weapon.

"Wanna bet who wins?" she asked him, and he melted away again.

From there, she followed the strong vibration of bass, the scent of heavy perfume, and the ocean surf roar of voices.

The lights here were red as well, with some smoke blue, fog gray shimmered in. Mists curled and crawled over the floor. The doorway was an arch, to represent the mouth of a cave. Over the arch the word BLOODBATH throbbed in bloody red.

Two bouncers, one black, one white, both built like tanked jets, flanked the arch, then stepped together to form a wall of oiled muscle.

"Invitation or passcode," they said in unison.

"This is both." Eve pulled out her badge, and got twin smirks.

"That doesn't mean jack down here," the one on the left told her. "Private club."

Before she could speak again, Roarke simply pulled out several bills. "I believe this is the passcode."

After the money passed, the bouncers separated to make an opening. As they walked through, Eve shot Roarke an annoyed look. "I don't have to bribe my way in."

**166**

"No, but you were going to hurt them, and that's a lot messier. In any case, it was worth the fee as you take me to the most interesting places."

The club was three open levels, dark and smoky, with the pentagram bar as the center. A stage jutted out on the second level where a band played the kind of music that bashed into the chest like hurled stones. Fog crept over it like writhing snakes. Patrons sat at the bar, at metal tables, lurked in corners or danced on platforms. Nearly all wore black, and nearly all were well under thirty.

There were some privacy booths and some were already occupied with couples or small groups smoking what was likely illegal substances inside the domes, or groping each other. Eve's gaze tracked up to note there were private rooms on the third level. The club had a live sex license, and no doubt all manner of acts transpired behind the doors.

She approached the bar where a man or woman worked at every point of the pentagram. Eve chose a woman with straight black hair parted in the center to frame a pale, pale face. Her lips were heavy and full and dyed deep, dark red.

"What can I get you?" the woman asked.

"Whoever's in charge." Eve set her badge on the slick black metal of the bar.

"There a problem?"

"There will be if you don't get me whoever runs this place."

"Sure." The bartender drew a headset out of her pocket. "Dorian? Allesseria. I've got a cop at station three asking for the manager. Sure thing."

She put the headset away again. "He'll be right down. Said I should offer you a drink, on the house."

"No, thanks. Have you seen this woman in here, Allesseria?" Eve drew out Tiara's ID photo.

She saw recognition immediately, then the quick wariness. And then the lie. "Can't say I have. We get slammed in here by midnight. Hard to pick out faces in the crowd, and with this lighting."

"Right. You got anything on tap here but beer and brew?"

Once again, Eve saw the lie. "I don't know what you mean. I just run the stick at this station. That's it, that's all. I got customers."

"She's not only a poor liar," Roarke observed. "She's a frightened one."

"Yeah, she is." Eve scanned the crowd again. She saw a man barely old enough to make legal limit actually wearing a cape, and a woman, nearly a decade older, all but bursting out of a long, tight black dress, who was wrapping herself around him like a snake on one of the dance platforms.

Another woman in sharp red sat alone in a privacy booth and looked mildly bored. When a man wearing mostly tattoos glided up to the bar, ordered, Allesseria poured something into a tall glass that bubbled and smoked. He downed it where he stood, throat rippling, then set the glass down with a snarling grin that flashed pointed incisors.

Eve literally felt Peabody shudder beside her. "Jesus, this place is creepy."

"It's a bunch of show and theater."

Then Eve saw him coming down the corkscrew of steps from the top level. He was dressed in black, as would be expected. His hair, black as well, rained past his shoulders, a sharp contrast to the white skin of his face. And that face had a hard and sensual beauty that compelled the eye.

He moved gracefully, a lithe black cat. As he reached the second level, a blonde rushed toward him, gripped his hand. There was a pathetic desperation about her as she leaned into him. He simply trailed his fingers down her cheek, shook his head. Then he bent to capture her mouth in a deep kiss as his hands slid under her short skirt to rub naked, exposed flesh. She clung to him afterward so that he had to set her aside, which he did by lifting her a foot off the ground in a show of careless strength.

Eve could see her mouth move, knew the woman called to him, though the music and voices drowned out the sound.

He crossed the main level, and his eyes locked with Eve's. She felt the jolt — she could admit it. His eyes were like ink, deep and dark and hooded. As he walked to her, his lips curved in a smile that was both knowing and confident.

And in the smile she saw something that didn't cause that quick, physical jolt, but a deep and churning physical dread.

"Good evening," he said in a voice that carried a trace of some Eastern European accent. "I'm Dorian Vadim, and this is my place."

Though her throat had gone dry, Eve gave him an acknowledging nod. "Lieutenant Dallas." She drew out her badge yet again. "Detectives Peabody and McNab. And . . ."

"No introduction necessary." There was another quality to him now, what seemed to be a prickly combination of admiration and envy. "I'm aware of Roarke, and of you, Lieutenant. Welcome to Bloodbath."

# CHAPTER
# FIVE

She knew what she saw when she looked at him. She saw in those pitch-dark eyes her greatest single fear: She saw her father.

There was no physical resemblance between the man before her and the one who had tormented and abused her for the first eight years of her life. It went, she understood, deeper than physical. Its surface was a calculated charm thinly coated over an indifferent cruelty.

Under it all was utter disregard for anything approaching the human code.

The monster that had lived in her father looked at her now out of Dorian Vadim's eyes.

And he smiled almost as if he knew it. "It's an honor to have you here. What can I get you to drink?"

"We're not drinking," Eve told him, though she would have paid any price but pride for a sip of water to cool the burning in her throat. "This isn't a social call."

"No, of course not. Well then, what can I do for you?"

Eve slid the photo of Tiara across the bar. Dorian lifted it, glanced at it briefly. "Tiara Kent. I heard she was killed this morning. Tragic." He tossed it down again without another glance. "So young, so lovely."

"She's been in here."

"Yes." He affirmed without an instant's hesitation. "A week or two ago. Twice, I believe. I greeted her myself when I was told she'd come in. Good for business."

"How did she get the invitation?" Eve demanded.

"One may have been sent to her. A selection of the young, high-profile clubbers is sent invitations periodically. We've only been open a few weeks. But as you can see ..." He turned, gestured to the crowd that screamed over the blasting music. "Business is good."

"She came alone."

"I believe she did, now that you mention it." He turned back, angling just a little closer to Eve, until the hairs on the back of her neck prickled. "As I recall, she was to meet a friend, or friends. I don't believe she did. I'd hoped she'd come back, with some of her crowd. They spend lavishly, and can make a club such as this."

"Underground clubs aren't made that way."

"Things change." He picked up the drink Allesseria had set on the bar, watching Eve over the rim as he sipped. "As do times."

"And how much time did you spend with Kent?"

"Quite a bit on her initial visit. I gave her a tour of the place, bought her a few drinks." He sipped again, slowly. "Danced with her."

Her father had smelled of candy from the mints he chewed to cover the liquor. Dorian smelled of musk, yet

**172**

she scented the hard sweetness of candy and whiskey. "Went home with her?"

He smiled, and when he set down his glass his knuckles lightly brushed Eve's hand. "If you want to know if I fucked her, you've only to ask. I didn't, though it was tempting. But bad for business. Wouldn't you agree?" he said to Roarke. "Sex with clients is a tricky business."

"It would depend on the client, and the business." Roarke's voice was a silky purr, a tone Eve knew was dangerous. "Other things are bad for business as well."

As if acknowledging some unspoken warning, Dorian angled his head in a slight nod, shifted his body away from Eve's.

"Did you tell her you were a vampire?" Eve demanded. "That you could turn her?"

Dorian slid on a stool and laughed. "Yes, to the first. It's part of the atmosphere, as you can clearly see. The core clientele come here for the thrill, the eroticism of the cult, the thrill of possibility. Certainly part of the draw is the fear and the allure of the undead, along with the dark promise of eternal youth and power."

"So you sell it, but you don't buy it."

"We'll just say I very much enjoy my work."

"Tiara Kent was exsanguinated, through a two-pronged wound through the carotid artery."

He lifted one arched black brow. "Really? Fascinating. Do you believe in vampires, Lieutenant Dallas? In those who prey on the human, and thirst for their blood?"

"I believe in the susceptible, in the foolish, and in those who exploit them. She was drugged first." Eve took a careless glance around and hated, *hated* that her chest felt tight. "I wonder how many illegals I'd net if I ordered a sweep of this place?"

"I couldn't say. We both know such things aren't as . . . regulated underground." He stared deeply into her eyes. "Just as we both know that's not what you're here for."

"One leads to another. Her killer left his DNA behind."

"Ah, well. We can, at least, settle that one particular element." Watching her still, he rolled up his sleeve. "Allesseria, I'll need a syringe with a vial. Unopened."

"You keep needles behind the bar?" Eve snapped out.

"Part of the show. We serve several drinks that contain a dram or two of pig's blood, and it's added with a syringe for flourish." He took the needle from the bartender. "Should you do the honors," he asked Eve, "or I?"

"A swab of your spit would be easier."

"But not nearly as interesting." He pumped his fist until a vein rose, then slid the needle neatly — expertly, Eve thought — into it. Depressed the plunger. "Allesseria, you'll witness I'm providing the lieutenant with my blood voluntarily."

When the bartender didn't speak, Dorian turned his head toward her slowly, stared.

"Yes. Yes, I will."

174

"That should be enough." He flashed a hard smile at Eve, then removed the needle, capped off the vial. "Thank you, Allesseria." Flipping the syringe agilely, he held it out, plunger first. "Dispose of that properly," he ordered, then handed the vial to Eve. "You'll mark and seal that in our presence?"

As she did, Dorian swiped his fingertip over the drop of blood on the tiny puncture in his flesh, then laid it on his tongue. "Is there anything else?"

"Did you see Miss Kent with anyone in particular, see her leaving with anyone?"

"I can't say I did. I believe she danced with any number of people. Feel free to ask any of the staff, and I'll be happy to ask myself."

"You do that. We'll need an address, Mr Vadim."

"Dorian, please. I'm known as Dorian. I can be reached here. I'm living upstairs at the moment. Let me give you a card." He waved his fingers, flicked them, and a glossy black card appeared between the index and middle finger. As he passed it to Eve, his fingers brushed down her palm, lingered for just an instant too long. Then he smiled. "I tend to sleep days."

"I bet. One more thing. Can you verify your whereabouts from midnight to three this morning?"

"I would have been here. As I said, I'm most often here."

"Anybody vouch for that?"

His lips quirked again, in a kind of smug amusement that put her back up. "I imagine so. You might ask any of the staff or the regulars. Allesseria?" He turned his black gaze from Eve's face to the bartender. "You were

175

on last night. Didn't we speak some time after midnight?"

"I was on until two." Allesseria kept her eyes locked on Dorian's. "You were, ah, working the floor before I left, came by the bar for a spring water just before I clocked out. At two."

"There you are. Lieutenant, it's been a pleasure." He took her hand, held it firmly. "But I really need to get back to work. Roarke. I hope you'll both come back, for the entertainment."

Through the fog that shimmered and curled, he glided off again, easing his way through the crowd. Eve shifted her body, stared hard at the bartender. "You want to tell me why you lied for him?"

"I don't know what you're talking about." Busily now, Allesseria wiped the bar.

"You don't see a woman whose face is all over the screen and mags, and she comes in at least twice, hangs with your boss. You don't make her." Some of the anger she felt for herself snapped out in her voice. "But you remember Dorian got a spring water at two in the morning."

"That's right."

"I need your full name."

"You're going to cost me my job if you don't back off."

"Full name," Eve repeated.

"Allesseria Carter. If you have any more questions, I'm calling a lawyer."

"That'll do it for now. You remember anything, get in touch." Eve laid one of her cards on the bar before she stepped away. "If that wasn't Kent's Prince of frigging Darkness pigs are currently dive-bombing Fifth Avenue."

"Blood will tell," Roarke said quietly.

"Bet your fine ass."

Once they were out on the street, Peabody's sigh was long and heartfelt. "Man. Creepshow — even if the Lord of the Undead is intensely sexy."

"Looked like another freak to me," McNab muttered.

"You're a guy who likes women. If you were a woman who liked men, we'd still be rolling your tongue back into your mouth. He completely smoked, right, Dallas?"

Women had found her father attractive, Eve thought. No matter what he'd done to them.

"I'm sure Tiara Kent thought the same even as he was draining the life out of her. I'm going to call a black-and-white for you. I want you to take the blood sample directly to the lab, wait while it's logged in."

"Got it." Peabody took the sample, stowed it in her bag.

"I'll run our host, and the bartender. This isn't his first time around the block — and she was lying about seeing him this morning. Lab comes through quickly enough, we'll be giving Vadim a very unpleasant wake-up call."

They separated, and as she walked Eve gave Roarke a quick hip bump. Now that she was on the street, away from Vadim, away from those pulsing lights, she felt herself again. "You're quiet."

"Contemplating. He was scoping you, you know. Subtle but quite deliberate." When she started to jam her hands into her pockets, Roarke took one, brought it casually to his lips. "He wanted to see your reaction — and mine."

"Must be disappointed we didn't give him one. Or much of one on your part."

"More puzzled, I'd think."

"Okay, why didn't you slap him back?"

"It was tempting, but more satisfying to let him wonder. In any case, he's not your type."

She snorted. "Nah. I don't go for the tall, dark, gorgeous types who exude sexuality like breath."

"You don't go for sociopaths."

She glanced up at him. He'd seen it, too, she realized. He'd seen at least that much, too. "You got that right."

"Besides, I'm taller."

Now she laughed, and because really, what did it hurt, she turned as she climbed the platform to the car, feigned judging his height as she laid her hands on his shoulders. She pressed her lips to his, warm, ripe, real, then eased back. "Yeah, I'd say you're exactly tall enough to fit my requirements. You drive, ace. I want to start the runs on the way home."

She used her PPC, and though it was limited to a miniscreen, Dorian Vadim's ID photo still had punch. His hair had been shorter when it was taken, but it still brushed past his shoulders. It listed his age at thirty-eight, his birthplace as Budapest, where according to his data, he still had a mother.

It also listed a very impressive sheet.

"Grifting's a specialty of our suave Mister V," Eve related. "Lotsa pops there, starting with a juvie record that was never sealed. Bounced around Europe and came to the States, it seems, in his early twenties. Arrests for smuggling — no convictions on that. Illegals, some pops, some questioned and released. Worked as an entertainer — mesmerist and magician. Hmmm. A lot of dropped charges, heavy on the female vics. Was questioned about the disappearance of two women he reputedly bilked. Not enough evidence to arrest, and no DNA in his records.

"Slithered through the system like a snake," she muttered. "No violence on record, but wits recant or poof with regularity." She frowned over at Roarke. "You buy into that mesmo stuff?"

"Hypnotism is a proven art, you know Mira uses it in therapy."

"Yeah, but mostly I think it's bull." Still she remembered the odd sensation she'd felt when Dorian had stared into her eyes. Her problem, she told herself. Her personal demons.

"Anyway, the man's bad news. And he's got a pattern of victimizing women, wealthy ones particularly."

She did a quick run on the bartender and found no criminal on Allesseria. "Bartender's clean. Divorced, with a kid just turning three." Eve pursed her lips as Roarke drove through the open gates toward home. "I get her in the box, even alone at her own place, I can break her. She's lying about seeing Dorian. I could snap her statement in five minutes without him around. He scares her."

"He's a killer."

"Yeah, no question."

"I mean she knows it, or believes it. You're capable of snapping her statement, and he's equally capable of snapping her neck — and with a great deal less passion."

"Wouldn't disagree. I just wonder why you'd say that after one conversation with him."

"I would have said it after one look at him. His eyes. He's a vampire."

Her mouth dropped open as he stopped the car. She hadn't managed to get words working with her thoughts until she'd pushed out of the car, rounded the hood to meet him. "You said what?"

"I mean it literally. His type sucks the life out of people, and does it for momentary pleasure, just as effectively as any fictional vampire. And he's just, darling Eve, as soulless."

Like her father, Eve thought. Yes, Roarke had seen it, too. He'd seen all of it. There was nothing strange or frightening about recognizing a monster.

It only meant she understood her quarry.

Eve stepped in, pulled off her jacket. She gestured toward Summerset, Roarke's majordomo, who — as he inevitably did — stood waiting in the foyer in his funereal black suit. "I always figured vampires looked like that. Pale, bony, dour, and dead." She tossed the jacket on the newel and started up the stairs.

"Will you be having dinner in the dining room like normal human beings this evening?" Summerset asked.

"Got work, and nobody who looks like you should toss around words like 'normal'."

"We'll get something upstairs," Roarke said placidly.

He strolled with Eve into her office, then immediately whipped around and boxed her against the wall. "I think I'll start with an appetizer," he said, then crushed his lips to hers.

Her blood went to instant sizzle. She could all but feel her brains leaking out of her ears as his mouth ravaged hers with a kind of feral impatience that thrilled. Even as she gripped his hips, he was doing torturous things to her body with those quick and clever hands.

She gulped in air, and simply gave herself to the wild and wanton moment. And to him.

She would always give. He knew no matter how much he wanted, she would always be there to give, or take, to meet those endless, urgent needs with her own. Her mouth was a fever on his. A moan poured from her as he tugged her shirt apart, then found that warm, trembling flesh with his lips, his teeth.

The taste of her incited a fresh and mammoth wave of hunger.

Her hands yanked at the hook of his trousers as his yanked at hers. And she pressed erotically against him, core to core.

Her eyes were dark when he looked into them and, for one brilliant moment, went blind when he plunged inside her.

She matched him, beat for frantic beat, riding and racing the violent pleasure as he dragged her arms over her head, as he pinned them there. As he battered them both over the last turbulent crest.

Her breath whistled in and out; he rested his cheek on her hair as he caught his own. And in sweet opposition to the force of their mating, he brushed his lips at her temple, soft as gossamer wings.

"I believe I was a bit more than mildly annoyed by having some poster boy for Dracula hit on my wife in front of my face."

"Worked for me." Grateful for the wall behind her, Eve leaned back, managed to focus on Roarke's eyes. "Feel better?"

"Considerably, thanks."

"Anytime. You know what, I feel like a big, fat hunk of red meat. How about you?"

He smiled, touched his lips to hers. "I could eat."

# CHAPTER
## SIX

She had an enormous hamburger while she backtracked through Dorian Vadim's criminal record. She burned up the 'link as she ate, as Dorian hadn't just slithered through the system, but had wound his way around the country and in and out of Europe while he did so. She spoke to detectives and investigators in Chicago, Boston, Miami, New L.A., East Washington, and several European cities.

She took copious notes, requested files, and made promises to keep other cops in other cities in the loop.

At some point during the process, Roarke wandered out. She'd set up another murder board, typed up her notes, and was talking to the head of security at Tiara Kent's building when Roarke wandered back in again.

She held up a finger.

"Go back as far as you can. If you see this guy on any of your discs, at any point, I want to know. Yeah, day or night. Thanks."

She disconnected. "Gist from the cops I've talked to across the frigging globe is Vadim is a smart grifter with the conscience and agility of a snake, an ego as big as . . . how big is Idaho?"

"There are bigger," Roarke considered, "but I'd say that's big enough."

"Okay, we'll go with Idaho, and an appetite for rich females and illegal substances. I'm damned if he'll slip through my fingers. Going to wrap him up quick, going to wrap him up tight," she told Roarke. "If we get him on any of the building's security discs, it's one more — ha, ha — nail in his coffin."

"Then you might be interested in what I ferreted out, regarding his financials."

Her expression went from intent to annoyed. "I don't have authorization to ferret in his financials, as yet."

"Which is why I used the unregistered. I don't like him," Roarke said very clearly before Eve could complain.

"Yeah, loud and clear on that. But I don't need his financial data at this point, and I can't use anything you found by illegal means, so —"

"So don't use it. And if you're not as curious as I was, I'll keep the information to myself."

He walked over, opened a wall panel, and got out the brandy. She lasted until he'd poured himself a snifter.

"Damn it. What did you find?"

"He's not officially listed as the owner of the club, but he owns it — such as it is. He's built several fronts, and is registered as its manager."

"Shady," she commented, "but not strictly illegal."

"He's also sunk quite a bit into the club — more, in my opinion, than makes good business sense on an underground establishment. I'd say Idaho might be lacking in square miles, after all. His overhead's

184

considerably more than his take, particularly considering his payroll."

"You hacked into his books for Bloodbath?"

"It wasn't any trouble." He swirled, then sipped
brandy. "Not much of a challenge. He's losing money
on it, every week. Yet his personal finances don't reflect
that. Instead there's a nice steady build. Nothing that
would wave flags, which tells me he's very likely tucked
away other accounts. I only scraped off a few layers on
this run."

"What's his other income?" Eve wondered, and
Roarke smiled.

"That's a question."

"Illegals are likely one chute. Bilking, blackmail,
extortion. Once a grifter . . . He could've been milking
Kent, but if it was just about money, why kill the really
rich cow before she runs dry? It's not just about
money," she said before Roarke could. "That's a shiny
side benefit."

"Agreed. And I'm going to wager very shiny. I can
take a hard look at Kent's finances, but I suspect she
was the type who flung money about like confetti on
New Year's Eve."

"Yeah, she had hundreds of shoes."

"I don't see the correlation, however," he continued
as she rolled her eyes. "With enough time, I could find
his hidey-holes, and jibe any unusual income with the
same outlay from Kent's."

"Given enough time," Eve repeated. "Hours or
days?"

"From the subjects in question, it could take a few days."

"Crap. Poking there won't hurt. But that's not what's going to get him."

"Again, we agree." He strolled over, sat on her desk. He liked it there, where he could look down into those whiskey-toned eyes. Those cop's eyes. "It may be weight, but it won't be your hammer. And as for the club, he's certainly got a second set of books on that, one that includes any exorbitant, and likely illegal membership fees, illegals transactions, and the like. Which I'll find for you, in time, as well."

"You're really handy to have around." She tapped his knee with her finger. "And not just for the sex."

"Darling, how sweet. I'll say the same of you." He bent down to kiss her lightly — another reason he liked sitting in just that spot. "On Vadim, if he were smarter, he'd be keeping his income and outlay closer on his official records. But he's not as smart as he thinks he is."

"But you're smarter than even he thinks he is." She paused, thought that through. "If you get me."

"Aren't we full of compliments tonight? I'll have to bang you against the wall more often."

She laughed, then picked up her coffee. She drank it even though it had gone cold. "I'll have the DNA match in the morning, maybe get lucky and get a blip of him on Kent's building's security. I'm going to corner the bartender and break down her corroboration of his bullshit alibi. I'll have him in a cage by noon.

Then we can take his finances and his records apart, piece by piece. You can add weight to my hammer."

Roarke angled his head. "Except? I can hear an 'except' in your voice."

"Except it's too easy, Roarke. It's all too goddamn easy on his end. He gave up his blood without a blink, and with a smile."

"I particularly dislike his smile," Roarke commented.

"Yeah? With you on that. He has to know he left DNA at Kent's that can hang him, but he didn't demand I get a warrant. And the fact is, it might have taken me some fast talking to get one for it. He may not be as smart as he thinks, but he's not stupid either. He's not worried, and that worries me."

"So, he has an ace in the hole somewhere. You'll just have to trump it. Now, tell me, what else is it that worries you?"

"I don't know what you mean."

"You went somewhere else in your head once or twice when we were in the club. And you've been there again a time or two since. Where did you go that worries you?"

"I've got a lot to push through, think through," she began.

"Eve." It was all he said. All he needed to say.

"I saw my father. I stood there in that ugly place, and he came toward me. Toward me," she repeated. "Not us, not the group of us, but me."

"Yes. Yes, he did."

"Like a dream, in a way. The fog, the lights, the noise. I knew it was for effect, for show, but . . . I got a hook in me, I guess, and then I looked in his eyes. You said sociopath. You said killer. And yeah, I saw that. But I saw more than that. When I looked into him I saw whatever monster it was that lived in my father. I saw it staring out at me. And it . . . it sickens me. It scares me."

Roarke reached down, took her hand. "Knowing monsters exist, as you and I do, Eve, may not always make for easy sleep, or even an easy heart. But it arms us against them."

"It was like he knew." She tightened her grip on his hand. There was no one else she could have told such things to. There had been a time when there'd been no one at all she could have told such things to. "I know it was my imagination, my own . . . demons, I guess you could say, but when he stared back into me, it was like he knew. Like he could see what was small and scared inside of me."

"You're wrong on that. What he saw was a woman who won't stand down."

"I hope so, because for a couple seconds I wanted to run. Just rabbit the hell out of there." She let out a shaky breath. "There are all kinds of vampires, you said that, too. Isn't that what my father was? Trying to suck the life out of me, trying to make me into something less than human? I put a knife into him instead of a stake. Maybe that's why he keeps coming back in my head."

"It's you who made you." He leaned down now, framed her face with his hands. "And what you are your father would never have understood. Neither would

**188**

Vadim. No matter how he looks, he'll never really see you."

"He thinks he does."

"His mistake. Eve, do you want to talk to Mira about this?"

"No." She considered it another moment, then shook her head and repeated, "No, not now anyway. Dumping on you levels it out a little. Taking him down, all the way down — that'll take care of the rest."

For a moment she studied their joined hands, then shifted her gaze up to his. "I didn't want to tell you I'd been scared, much less why. I guess that was stupid."

"It was."

She scowled. "Aren't you supposed to say something like 'No, it wasn't. Blah, blah, support, stroke, let me get you some chocolate'?"

"You haven't read the marriage handbook, footnotes. It's another woman who does that sort of thing. I believe I'm allowed to be more blunt, then ask if you'd like a quick shag."

"Shag yourself," she said and made him laugh. "But thanks anyway."

"Offer's always on the table."

"Yeah, yeah, and the floor, in the closet, or on the front stairs. Time to work, ace, not to play."

She pushed up to study and circle her murder board, and he knew she was soothed and settled.

"Prior bad acts, and plenty of them. Mysterious income. Contact with the vic, and the profile fits him like a tailor-made suit. Bullshit alibi. He's running a game in that club, skinning rich idiots with his vampire fantasy, maybe blackmailing them, selling illegals. But that's only part of the picture. He's got something," she said in a mutter now. "He's got something, and he's feeling fucking smug about it."

"Heads up, Lieutenant," Roarke warned.

She glanced his way, caught the candy bar he tossed across the room. She grinned, tore the wrapper, and biting in, continued to study her board.

When Allesseria finished her shift, she was careful not to rush, careful to do everything just as she did every night. She closed down her tabs, keyed in her codes, passed her station off to her replacement.

She stretched her back as she walked, casually, to the employee-only area where she stowed her bag and her jacket every shift. Even there, behind closed doors, she kept her expression neutral and her movements routine. Everyone knew there were cameras in every section of the club, the boss had made that clear.

You never knew who was watching.

Her yawn wasn't entirely feigned. It had been a long shift, and a busy one as the crowds that patronized Bloodbath liked to stay thoroughly lubed. As she always did, she transferred her tips to her bag, zipped them into its inside pocket. After fitting the bag's strap across her body, she put her jacket over it.

She hung the illuminated cards, given to all employees, around her neck so that one glowed between her breasts, the other between her shoulder blades.

With the gleaming gold pentagram with its boldly red double B's in the center like a shield front and

**190**

back, nobody would bother her on the way out of the club, on the nasty route through the tunnels. It was something else Dorian had made clear from the get-go, and he'd made an example of a souped-up chemi-head who'd tried a move on one of the waitresses the first week the club opened.

Rumor was the guy had ended up in pieces, and there hadn't been enough blood left to so much as stain the ground.

It was probably bullshit. Probably. But it was enough to keep the path clear for anyone coming or going from Bloodbath who wore the sign.

Still, she checked her pocket, as she always did, for her ministunner and panic button.

An ounce of prevention was worth a lot of peace of mind.

She headed out, and as was usual at shift changes, she left the club with a group of other employees. Safety in numbers. There wasn't much chatter, there rarely was, so she could huddle inside her own thoughts as they wound through the stink and the shadows, through the pounding music and wailing screams.

She'd thought she could handle it, the money was too good to pass up. With salary and tips, if she was frugal, she could move out of the city, plunk down a down payment on a nice little house.

A yard for her kid, a day job.

It seemed like the perfect plan, and she knew how to take care of herself. But it was too much, she had to face that now. The club, the tunnels, the boss himself. It was all too much, and she was going to have to go back to working street level, pulling doubles just to put a few extra aside every week. The house in Queens, the yard, the dog, would all just have to wait a few more years.

She'd walked out of Bloodbath for the last time.

She'd send in written notice, that's what she'd do, Allesseria decided as she finally came out to the sidewalk. She'd use her son as an excuse. Dorian knew she had joint custody, but she could use the night work as too strenuous, too difficult.

Nothing he could do about it, she assured herself as she pulled off the glowing cards and stuffed them in her pocket. Nothing, that she could think of, that he'd want to do. At the salary he offered, he'd replace her in one crook of the finger.

Let somebody else mix pig's blood — God, she *hoped* it was just pig's blood — in gin to make Bloody Martinis, or handle dry ice to make a Graveyard. She was done.

The cops had been the last straw. She couldn't take any more.

He'd made her lie for him, so there was a reason he needed the lie.

As Allesseria went underground again, this time to catch the subway home, she admitted she'd lied before he'd asked. Something had warned her she'd be better off playing dumb.

Never seen that face before.

Tiara Kent, who'd knocked back a half-dozen Bloodies on her first visit to the club — and had spent a hell of a lot of time up in Dorian's private office.

Okay, she hadn't seen them leave together, but in fact, she hadn't seen either of them leave when Tiara had come to the club. Which meant they might have slipped out through Dorian's office.

And Allesseria hadn't seen Dorian from sometime before midnight last shift. He hadn't come down to work the floor as she'd told the cop he had. He hadn't worked the floor, not once that she'd noticed, after Tiara Kent had gone up those stairs with him.

And she always noticed him because of the way her skin started to crawl.

He could've killed Tiara Kent. He could've done it.

With her arms protectively crossed over her torso, Allesseria sat on the train, struggling with what she should do, could do. A dozen times she told herself just walking away was enough. It wasn't her responsibility, and she'd be smarter to just mind her own business. Quitting was enough. More than enough.

But when she got off at her stop, she thought of her son, how she tried to teach him to do the right thing, to stand up for what he knew was right. To be a good man one day.

So she pulled out the card the cop had left on the bar and her pocket 'link as she walked the dark street home.

Nerves prickled at the base of her spine, crawled up to the back of her throat. Even though she told herself it was foolish, she shot anxious glances over her shoulder. Nothing to worry about now, *nothing*. She was blocks from the club, and back on street level. As far as Dorian knew she'd backed him up, 100 percent.

She was nearly home. She was safe.

Still, she stayed in the streetlights where she could as she recited Eve's office code. When she reached voice mail, she took a long breath.

"Lieutenant Dallas, this is Allesseria Carter, the bartender at Bloodbath."

She paused, looking over her shoulder again as those nerves dug in like claws. Had she heard something? Footsteps, a rustle in the breeze?

But she saw nothing but light and shadow, the black, blank windows in the buildings.

Still, she increased her pace, felt her knees tremble as she hurried. "I need to talk to you, um, talk to you about Tiara Kent. If you could contact me as soon —"

He came out of nowhere, charging in like some dark and brutal wind. Shock had her sucking in air as she whirled around, as she stumbled back. She managed one choked-off scream as his hand closed over her throat, squeezing out even that single panicked gulp. The black eyes stared into hers when her 'link went flying. As if she weighed nothing at all, he lifted her off the ground.

"You," he said in a quiet, almost pleasant tone, "made a very tragic mistake."

She kicked, her legs dancing and dangling like a hanging man's when he dragged her out of the circle of light from the street lamp. Red dots exploded in front of her eyes while her lungs screamed for air and her hand fumbled wildly for her panic button.

Her feet thudded on broken steps, and tears spurted out of her eyes. They bulged in horror when he smiled and she saw, impossibly, the flash of fangs.

In the dark, those gleaming points sank into her neck.

The minute she was dressed in the morning, Eve snagged a second cup of coffee. "I'm going to check my home office machine, see if I got anything from the lab overnight."

"Being a bit obsessive, aren't you?" Roarke asked from where he sat, scanning the morning financials on the bedroom screen. "It's barely seven."

"You have your obsessions." She nodded toward the maze of numbers. "I have mine."

"Check it from your pocket 'link then. Have something to eat while you're about it."

"How am I supposed to check my office messages with my pocket 'link?"

Roarke only sighed, rose. He walked to her and held out a hand. "They're all connected, my technology-challenged darling, hence the term '*link*."

"Yeah, yeah, but then you have to remember all these codes and sequences, and it's just easier to . . ."

He punched a command while she frowned at him. "Relay any new incomings on home unit Dallas," he ordered.

Acknowledged . . . There are no incomings
since last operator use on home unit Dallas . . .

"Huh. Okay, not as complicated as I thought. Can I check my unit at Central?"

He only smiled. "Relay any new incomings on office unit Dallas, Cop Central."

Acknowledged . . . There is one new incoming transmission on voicemail . . .

"Damn it." She grabbed the 'link out of Roarke's hand. "I told them to contact me here as soon as they had —"

*Lieutenant Dallas, this is Allesseria Carter, the bartender at Bloodbath.*

"Conscience got to her," Eve decided, watching the face on screen. "Walking home, it looks like. Looks spooked."

*I need to talk to you, um, talk to you about Tiara Kent. If you could contact me as soon —*

There was a sound — a rush of wind? Eve saw a black-gloved hand, the blur of it whip in and close over Allesseria's throat.

"Fuck! Goddamn it." Eve's own hand clamped on Roarke's arm as the screen image blurred, the 'link struck the sidewalk, and the display went black.

"Play it back again," she ordered Roarke as she yanked out her communicator. "Dispatch, Dallas, Lieutenant Eve. I need a unit, closest possible unit at . . ." She flipped quickly through her memory to the address she'd pulled out of Allesseria's data, then snapped it out. Repeated it. "Possible victim of assault is Carter, Allesseria. Female, Caucasian, thirty-four, black hair, medium build. I'm on my way."

"I'll go with you," Roarke told her. "I'm closer than Peabody. You can contact her on the way. You know you won't find her in her apartment," he added as they rushed downstairs.

"Maybe she got away. Maybe he just wanted to scare her. Goddamn it, I picked her out for him. I set her up."

"You did nothing of the kind." He snatched up her jacket from the newel, tossed it to her as he snagged his own. "He chose her, the minute he asked her to lie for him, he chose her. I'll drive."

He'd get there faster, Eve knew, and it freed her to contact Peabody, then take the report from Dispatch. There was no response at Allesseria's apartment.

"Get inside," Eve snapped. "The victim's life is in immediate jeopardy. I have probable cause. Get the fuck inside."

She thumped her fist against her leg as she waited, waited, as Roarke maneuvered her police-issue through streams and clogs of morning traffic.

Dispatch, Dallas, Lieutenant Eve. Officers report the apartment is currently unoccupied. There is no sign of break-in or foul play.

No, Eve thought, there wouldn't be. He didn't take her there. "Start an immediate search in a five-block radius. Repeating description. Subject is female,

Caucasian, age thirty-four, black and brown, last seen wearing black pants, black shirt, red jacket."

Eve ended the transmission, stared out the windshield. "I know it," she said, though Roarke had said nothing. "I know it. He didn't leave her alive."

# CHAPTER
# SEVEN

Eve scanned sidewalks, the buildings as they approached Allesseria's apartment. It was a tough, low end of the lower-middle-class neighborhood. Most self-respecting muggers would hunt for scores a few blocks away in any direction.

Pickings would be slim here, and the population willing to fight for what they carried in their pockets. Street level LCs would troll for Johns elsewhere, too. All in all, the handful of blocks were safe simply because they were poor enough not to warrant much trouble.

But Allesseria Carter hadn't been safe.

Eve's gaze zeroed in on a subway exit. "Pull over, park wherever you can. She'd take the subway, wouldn't she? Cheap and quick. If she did, this would've been her route home."

She slammed out of the car the minute Roarke stopped, then pulled out her 'link to replay the message. Looked for landmarks. "It's dark, and it's mostly her face, but . . ." She held up her own 'link as if relaying a message, then looked over her left shoulder. "See here, could be that building in the background."

She kept walking, studying the screen, the street. "Here, he took her right about here. Somebody would've picked up her 'link by now, or he did, but it was right about here he attacked."

She scanned again, focused on a narrow building sagging between a Thai market and a boarded-up storefront. It was plastered with graffiti, and what looked like an old, torn CONDEMNED sign.

Eve took out her communicator, requested backup at the location. Then drawing her weapon, she started toward the door. "You carrying anything besides half the wealth of the world in your pocket?"

"Burglary tools, though this won't require them."

She nodded, reached down, and took her clutch piece out of its ankle holster. "You're deputized, ace." She sucked in a breath, kicked in the door.

She went in low and to the right while he took high and left in a routine they'd danced before. Sunlight dribbled through the broken windows, striking off shards of glass, filth, vermin droppings.

And blood.

Eve could smell it — not just the blood, but the death. That heavy human stench.

Roarke took out a penlight, shone it on the trail of smeared red.

He'd left her splayed on the floor, arms and legs spread out so her body formed a gruesome human X. Most of her clothes had been torn off, leaving only ragged remnants of black clinging to skin mottled with bruises.

Her blood spread out in a pool from the puncture wounds in her throat. Her eyes hadn't lost their horror with death, but stared at the ceiling in a fixed expression of abject terror.

"Didn't take her blood with him this time," Eve said quietly. "Didn't come prepared for that. But he made sure to hurt her plenty before he bled her out. Got off on her pain, got off on the power. See how he spread her out? Motherfucker."

Roarke touched a hand to Eve's shoulder. "I'll get your field kit."

She worked the scene; it's what she did. What she had to do. She could follow the trail of blood, of smeared footprints, and see Allesseria being dragged inside.

Kicking, Eve thought, her work shoes thudding hard against the broken concrete steps. Hard enough to cut through the cheap canvas before he'd hauled her inside.

He'd punctured her throat immediately, only steps inside the door. There was spatter against the dirty wall where she'd gushed. Where she'd collapsed. Dragged her unconscious from there, she noted. Gave himself a little more room to work. To beat her with his fists, to rape her. All while the blood ran out of her.

But he'd taken some, too. Ingested it, bottled it. She'd find out.

"Time of death oh-three-thirty," she said for the record. "Took her about an hour to die." She sat back on her haunches. "A block and a half from home."

She looked over at Roarke. He stood, his hands in the pockets of his jacket. The morning air fluttered in the broken windows, stirred his dark hair. And lifted the smell of ugly death all around them.

"He could've taken her in the club, anywhere in the underground. She might never have been found, and we'd never prove a thing if she'd been murdered down there."

"He wanted you to find her," Roarke agreed. "He's making a statement."

"Yeah, oh, yeah, because he didn't have to do this. Even if she recants, he'd find ten others to back his alibi. Ten others he'd bribe or intimidate. He didn't have to kill her, and certainly not like this."

"He enjoyed it." Roarke shifted his gaze, met Eve's eyes. "Just as you said. Payback was secondary to the killing."

"And he wanted it to be me who found her," Eve added. "Because of that click last night, that mutual recognition. But he's too cocky for his own good. There'll be DNA again, and he'll have picked up some of this dirt. Shoes, clothes. He'll have transferred some of this dirt, this blood, and the sweepers will find it."

"He attacked her while she was on the 'link — to you, Eve." Reaching out, Roarke took her hand, lifted her to her feet. "That's another statement."

"Yeah, and I'm hearing him. Just like he's going to hear me, really soon." She looked over as Peabody came in.

"Nothing on the canvass so far," Peabody reported. "I got in touch with the ex-husband. He lives a few blocks from here. He's on his way."

"We'll take him outside. He doesn't need to see this."
Nobody needed to see what cops had to see. "Body can
be bagged and tagged. There's nothing else she can tell
us here. Let's see what she says to Morris."

She went out, grateful for the sunlight, and for the
smell that was New York rather than death. She started
to reach for her 'link to nag the lab yet again, when
she spotted a six-and-a-half-foot black man with a body
like a linebacker sprinting across the street against the
light.

He wore short dreads, sweatpants, and a T-shirt, and
an expression of fear in his topaz eyes. When he tried —
and was well on his way to succeeding — shoving past
the uniforms at the crime-scene barricade, she called
out, went over.

"Rick Sabo?"

"Yes. Yes. My wife — my ex-wife. A detective called
and said . . ."

"Let him through. I'm Lieutenant Dallas, Mr Sabo.
I'm sorry about your ex-wife."

"But are you absolutely sure it's her? She had a panic
button, a ministunner. She knew how to handle herself.
Maybe —"

"She's been identified, I'm sorry. When did you —"

She broke off when he just crouched down, dropped
his head in his hands as a man would if pierced by a
sudden and unspeakable pain. "Oh, God, oh, God.
*Alless*. I can't . . . I told her to quit that goddamn job.
I told her."

"Why did you tell her to quit her job?"

He looked up, but since he didn't straighten, Eve hunkered down with him. "She worked in this cult club — vampire shit — which is bad enough. But it was underground, off Times Square. It wasn't safe, it's not safe down there, and she knew it."

"Then why'd she work there?"

"Made three times what she made on street level. Sometimes four with tips. No doubles. She wanted to buy a house, a little house, maybe in Queens. We've got a boy." His eyes watered up. "We got Sam, and she wanted a place out of the city. We share custody of Sam. But, Jesus, I told her it wasn't worth it. I went down to check it out right after she took the job. Goddamn pit in a goddamn sewer. Alless."

There was love here, Eve thought. Maybe not enough to make a marriage work, but there was love. "Did she talk about her work, the people she worked with? For?"

"No, not to me. Not after we went a round about it. Haven't fought like that since we split. Don't know that we fought like that before we split. I was scared, if you want to know the truth. Scared for her, and I handled it wrong."

His hands dangled between his knees now, and he stared at them as if they were foreign objects. "Flat out told her she was *going* to quit, and I know that's just the way to make her dig into something. If I'd handled it better, she might've . . ."

He looked up, looked past Eve. There were people gathered on the other side of the barricades, as people always did.

204

*What happened?* they'd ask, and as word trickled down, they'd think how awful, how terrible, even as they continued to gawk, to linger, to hope to catch a glimpse of the dead body before they had to head off to work.

Because it wasn't them, it wasn't theirs the city had swallowed up. So they could gawk and linger and congratulate themselves that it wasn't them or theirs — and the next time it might be.

Sabo didn't see them, Eve knew that, too. Because for him, it was the next time.

"Mr Sabo, did you meet any of her coworkers or her employer while you were in the club, or after?"

"What? No. No." He scrubbed his hands hard over his face. "Didn't want to. I only stayed about twenty minutes. Illegals passing around like party favors. People coming out of the private rooms licking blood off their lips, or it looked like it. She wanted a damn house in Queens."

"Mr Sabo, I have to ask. It's routine. Can you verify your whereabouts between two and four A.M. this morning?"

"In bed, at home. I got Sam. I can't leave Sam alone at night." He rubbed at his eyes now before his hands dangled uselessly again. "I have building security. In and out. You can check. Whatever you have to do so you don't waste time, so you find who hurt Alless. Was she raped?"

Before Eve could respond, he shook his head. "No. No. Don't tell me. I don't think I want to know either way. Walk from the subway, after two in the morning, alone. Because of that damn job. Now what am I going to tell our boy? How am I going to tell our Sam his mama's gone?"

"I can have a grief counselor contact you, one who works with children."

"Yes. Please. Yes." His throat worked on a swallow. "I'll need help. Alless and I, well, we couldn't stay married, but we were a team when it came to Sam. I'll need help. I have to get back to my kid. I left him with the neighbor. I have to get back to Sam. Can you let me know when . . . when I need to do whatever I need to do?"

"We'll contact you, Mr Sabo." Eve watched him walk away. "Peabody?"

"I'll take care of the grief counselor. Poor guy."

"Murder kills more than the victim," Eve said quietly. "We need to wrap up here, get into Central. Feeney may be able to clean up some of her last transmission from my unit. We get even a glimmer of this bastard . . ."

"I could help with that." Roarke stepped up beside her.

"You've got your own work."

"I do, but I'd be interested in, let's say, hammering one of those nails."

"If Feeney —" She broke off as her 'link signalled. "Hold on a minute." She moved aside, answered.

Roarke noted the instant change in her body language — the stiffening, the aggressive stance. When she turned back, he saw it mirrored in the temper that heated her eyes.

"DNA doesn't match Vadim's."

"But —"

"No but about it," Eve cut Peabody off. "There's a fucking screwup somewhere. You want in," she said to Roarke, "you're in. You can round up Feeney at Central, do whatever the two of you can do with the transmission. Peabody, with me. We're going to the lab. Contact Morris." She moved quickly as she snapped out the order. "I want him to personally take the DNA samples from this vic, have them hand-delivered to the lab. That's red-flagged."

"Got it."

Eve glanced back at the building one last time. "No way, no goddamn way he slithers out of this."

Peabody had to all but leap into the car to keep up. "Maybe he didn't kill her."

"Screw that."

"What I mean is, maybe he had her killed. Set it up." Peabody jerked her safety harness tight as it looked like they were in for a hell of a ride.

"No. He wouldn't deny himself the pleasure of the kill." Monsters didn't want to watch, to be told. They wanted to do. They wanted the smell of the blood. "He did them both. Kent because it's what he set out to do, Carter because he was smart enough to know she wasn't going to hold up his alibi, and it slaps at me. He picked her, put her on the spot, then he took her out. The lab screwed up, or I did. I did if he switched the vials."

"We were right there. He drew his own blood right in front of us."

"Hand's quicker than the eye," Eve muttered. "He worked as a magician, he's worked the grift all of his life. He offered the blood sample without a blink because he knew he could swing it so it wouldn't match."

And she'd been distracted, she couldn't deny it. Tight chest, dry throat, pumping heart. Her own fears had dulled her senses.

"Either way," Peabody commented, "without the match, with Allesseria vouching for him and being unable to recant, we've got nothing on him."

"That's what he's counting on. I played into it, and that pisses me off. Dark club, all that movement and noise. Guy draws his own blood at a bar. Not something you see every day." Looking into his eyes, she remembered. Caught in them for a few seconds too long, shuddering inside at what she'd seen there, and she's conned. "Son of a bitch."

She strode into the lab, only to be cut off by the chief, Dick Berenski.

His egg-shaped head was cocked aggressively as he jabbed one of his long, thin fingers at her. "Don't think about coming into my shop and saying we fucked up. I ran those samples twice myself. Personal. You want to argue with science, you go somewhere else. I can't make a match when there's no match."

He was called Dickhead for a reason, and it had everything to do with his personality. Eve throttled back. "I think he switched them on me. It's his DNA on the vic, but it's not his in the vial you have. I've got an idea how he pulled it off, but the question right now is: If it's not his blood in the vial, whose is it?"

It was obvious Berenski had been expecting a battle. Now, caught off guard, he was more accommodating than he normally would be without a substantial bribe. "Well, if we got the DNA in the system, I can find it for you."

"I did a standard search, crapped out."

"Global?"

"Yeah, do I look like this is my first day on the job? But I didn't run deceased."

"Blood from a corpse? How's that going to end up in some mope's veins?"

"Not in his veins, in a damn vial he palmed off on me. Can you do a global search, deceased donor?"

"Sure."

"How fast?"

He wiggled his spidery fingers. "Watch and learn."

He went back to his station, the long white counter with comps and screens and command centers. Sliding back and forth on his stool, he began to work — verbal orders, manual keys.

While he ran the searches, Eve drew out her 'link and tried Feeney.

Her old partner and the captain of EDD popped on her screen. He had a Danish in one hand, and a mouth full of the hefty bite missing from it. "Yo."

"Roarke's on his way in. Put him to work. I've got a 'link trans, voice mail, from a vic while she was being attacked. Lost the trans almost as soon. It's dark, it's jumpy, but if you can clean it up, I might bum this bastard quick."

"Take a look." He swallowed. "This your vampire?"

"Come on."

"Hey, before your time I took down this asshole who was grave robbing, then sewing body parts together. Thought he could make himself a Frankenstein. Weird shit happens. He take another one?"

"Yeah, early this morning."

Contemplatively, Feeney took another bite of Danish. "McNab said he pulled out a syringe and gave you blood right on the spot."

"Yeah. There was a screwup there. Looks like mine. I'll fill you in later. Anything you can do on the trans, Feeney, I'd appreciate."

"Your man gets here, we'll do some magic. Meanwhile, you go up against this guy, wouldn't hurt to take a cross along." He lifted his eyebrows when she just stared at him. "Kid, weird shit happens because people are fucking crazy."

"I'll keep that in mind."

She clicked off just as Berenski made a sound of victory. "Got your blood. And I'm forced to say, 'Damn good call, Dallas'."

"I'm forced to say, 'Damn fast work'."

"I'm the best. Pensky, Gregor." He tapped the ID picture on his screen.

Square face, Eve noted. Small eyes, pinched mouth. The data put him at two-ten and six-one, with a long sheet of violent crimes.

It also listed him as dead for nearly a year.

"How'd he get to be a corpse?" Eve demanded.

"Son of a bitch." Berenski pursed his thin lips. "Been running DNA on a DB." He called for the data.

210

"Body found in the woods in freaking Bulgaria, where it was believed he headed after escaping from a work program on his latest visit to their version of the State Pen." Eve shook her head. "Work program for a guy with this kind of sheet. Bludgeoned, partially dismembered, and how about this, exsanguinated. Peabody, let's get the full ME's report on this. I'm betting among his other injuries, there were a couple of puncture wounds in his throat."

"This vampire shit's creepy."

Eve glanced at Berenski. "It would be, if vampires existed. What happened to science?"

He jutted out what he called a chin. "You got science, you got the para side of it. I'd be sharpening stakes if I were you, Dallas."

"Yeah, that's on my list."

"Really?" Peabody asked when they got back into the car.

"Really what?"

"The stake-sharpening detail."

"Peabody, you're making my eye twitch."

"I know it's out there, but you have to consider all the information. Blood from a corpse. Vampires are corpses, essentially. No trace of Vadim on the first vic, scientifically at this point in time."

"Because he switched the fucking vials."

"Okay, okay." Peabody held up both hands, palms out. "But if you bought into the vampire lore, he could've sired this Pensky guy, then —"

"Then his body wouldn't have been real available for the Bulgarian ME."

**211**

Peabody considered. "There's that. But do we know, for absolute *sure*, that it stayed available?"

Give up, Eve told herself. Logical debates can't be made out of illogical theorems. "You be sure to check on that. While you do, I'll just stick with the more pedestrian theory that Vadim hooked up with Pensky, killed the shit out of him, and stored the blood he drained out for later use. It's smart, but it would've been a hell of a lot smarter to get blood from some unknown. We're also going to see if we can pin Vadim's whereabouts for the time of this Gregor's murder. What do you bet he was in Bulgaria?"

"He'd've been in Bulgaria if he vamped him, too," Peabody said under her breath. "Guy's got devil eyes."

"On the last part we heartily agree." She pulled into the garage at Central. "And we're going to give him a shot right between them. All data on Gregor Pensky's autopsy, Vadim's whereabouts at the time in question — and last night. Another DNA sample from that slippery son of a bitch."

Mentally kicking herself one more time on that score, Eve slammed the door of her police-issue. "This one spit — and it's going to be taken by a certified criminalist. Going to wrap him up before the day ends. He's not going to bite anyone else."

"Dallas?" Peabody scrambled inside the elevator. "Do you figure he's fatally bitten someone before? Bulgaria's a long way from Times Square. And there are places farther away. Places where bodies might never be found." Even if, Peabody thought, they stayed buried.

"I don't think he took a year off between Pensky and Kent." Eve scowled at the elevator doors. "So yeah, I think there'll be others."

"So do I. And listen, whether or not you — I mean we — believe in vampires, who's to say he doesn't? I know how he played it at Bloodbath. Like it was a show, a con — but a legal one this time. Maybe it isn't."

"Mira's initial profile allowed for him deluding himself into believing himself immortal, but his sheet screams con. We get him in the box," Eve decided, "we'll see how he plays it."

"I'm thinking if he does believe it, he's feeling pretty full of himself right now. Sucking out two vics in two nights."

"As of now, he's going on a no-hemoglobin diet."

Inside Central, Eve turned toward the Homicide bullpen. Stopped. Swags of garlic hung from the door frame like some odd holiday decoration. She caught the snickers from up and down the corridor, decided to ignore them, just as she ignored the surreptitious glances shot her way when she walked inside.

She arrowed in on Baxter, strolled to his desk. "How much did it run you?"

"It's fake." He grinned at her. "I'd have sprung for real, even though it's steep, but it's hard to come by enough to make a real impact so we got the fake stuff, too. You gotta admit, it's funny."

"Yeah, inside I'm cracking up. I'm going back down to reinterview Count Dracula. Get your boy, you're backup."

"Underground." His grin vanished into a look of pure disgust. "I just bought these shoes."

"Now I'm crying on the inside." She pushed him aside with a satisfied grin, and commandeered Baxter's computer.

Moments later, her suspicions were confirmed. Two puncture wounds had pierced Gregor Pensky's carotid artery and had been attributed to an animal bite. She had news for Bulgaria, and the standing medical examiner. But for now, she contacted her own.

"What've you got?" she demanded of Morris.

"Saliva and semen, and I had my top man walk them to the lab. Exsanguination was COD. She was beaten pre- and postmortem, he used his fists on her, and wore gloves. Her larynx was partially crushed by manual strangulation. Tox just came back. Traces of the same cocktail inside Kent, administered through the neck wounds."

"He transferred the drug through the bite?"

"Yes. She didn't consume any blood, or alcohol."

"This one wasn't a party. Thanks, Morris." She sat back for a moment, organizing thoughts and strategy.

"Peabody," she said as she got to her feet. "Baxter, Trueheart. Let's move." She strode to the doorway, flicked a bulb of garlic with her finger. "You can take some of this along if that does it for you. Me?" She tapped her sidearm. "I'll stick with this."

214

# CHAPTER
# EIGHT

Baxter might like to joke, and bitch about damage to his slick wardrobe, but he was a solid cop. His uniformed aide, Trueheart, hadn't shaken off all the green, but he was dependable as sunrise.

There wasn't a cop on the job — or not a sane one — who would be thrilled to traverse underground, day or night. But there weren't any who would back her up more reliably.

She took point, left Baxter to take the rear. Below the streets, time vanished. In the world, the day was sunny and heading toward warm. Here, it was as dark and dank as midnight in a winter graveyard. Still, at this hour most of those who inhabited the tunnels were huddled away in their holes and burrows.

Some of the clubs and arcades ran 24/7, and the harsh music still pumped, the ugly lights still glared. Those who came or stayed to do business were more interested in the pain or gain than confronting four armed cops.

A few threats and insults were hurled. One brave soul invited *the girls* to have a taste of the appendage he was proud enough of to whip out and dangle in their direction.

Eve paused long enough to glance down. "Only thing down here interested in a taste of that is the rats, but they generally like bigger meals."

This comment caused hilarity among the flasher's companions.

"Sir," Peabody said, with feeling, "I really don't think you should tease the animals."

"The rats can handle it."

Eve turned down the next tunnel as the insulted flasher shouted inventive suggestions about what Eve might do with his pride and joy.

"Gotta give him points for originality," Baxter commented.

"And optimism," Trueheart added, and made his partner hoot with laughter.

Despite herself, Eve tossed a grin over her shoulder. His young, handsome face might have been pale and just a little clammy, but Trueheart was game.

The shouts echoed away as they reached Bloodbath. It was locked down tight.

She used the number Dorian had given her. With the video blocked, he answered in a slurred and sleepy voice.

"Dallas, official police business. Open up."

"Of course. One moment."

It took a bit longer than one, but the locks clicked, the security lights blinked to green. And the barred doors slid slowly open.

Eve saw the extra minutes had given Dorian time to set the stage.

**216**

Inside the lights were a dim and smoky blue with pulsing red undertones. The screen behind the stage flickered on, filled with images in black and white of women being attacked or willingly baring their necks for fangs. The blood that ran down flesh was black as pitch.

Dressed in black, his shirt open to the waist, Dorian stood above the screen on one of the open balconies. He seemed to float there on a thin river of fog, as if he could, at any moment, simply lift his arms and rise into the air. His face was ghost pale, his eyes and hair black as ink.

"I see you brought company." His voice flowed, echoed. "Please . . ." He gestured toward the steps. "Come up."

"That's a spider to the fly invite," Baxter murmured, glanced at Eve. "You go first."

She hated that her heart stuttered, that her blood ran cold under her skin. Though her stomach clenched in protest, she crossed the club floor where more fog was beginning to curl and snake, and her bootsteps echoed on the iron steps as she climbed.

Smiling, slowly smiling, Dorian stepped back. And vanished in the mist.

She drew her weapon. An instant later she had to fight not to jolt as he seemed to materialize directly in front of her. His eyes were so dark she couldn't tell pupil from iris. In them, if she let herself look, were all the horrors of her childhood.

"Nice trick," she said casually. "And a good way to get stunned."

"I trust your reflexes. My home." He gestured again, then led the way through an open door.

217

Black and red and silver. He'd played up the gothic touches, Eve noted, but didn't lack for plush. Iron chandeliers held white candles, wall niches showcased statuary of demons or nudes in pornographic poses.

There were curved black divans and black high-backed chairs studded with metal, and a single life-sized painting of a woman in a diaphanous white gown, bent limply over the arm of a black-caped man. Her eyes were wide with terror, her mouth open in a scream, as he bent toward her neck with fangs exposed.

"My humble home," Dorian said. "I hope you approve."

"A little too theatrical for my taste." She turned and looked him directly in the eyes. Eyes that triggered memories and fears she couldn't completely bury. "I'm going to need another sample, Dorian. I'll need you to come in for this one."

"Really? I'd think I gave you more than enough blood . . . for police purposes. A drink for you or your companions?"

"No."

"Excuse me while I get one. I'm not used to being up so early in the day." He moved to a bar, opened the minifridge behind it. He took out a squat black bottle, poured red and thick liquid into a silver cup.

"We'll arrange your transport, have you back for your morning nap."

"I'd like to oblige you, but it's just not possible." He gestured an apology with one hand. "I'm under no legal obligation, after all."

"We'll discuss that at Central."

**218**

"I don't think so." Carrying his cup, he walked to a desk. "I have here a document that lists me — quite legally — as unable to tolerate sunlight. Religious reasons." He passed the document to her. "As to the sample, I'm afraid you'll need a warrant this time. I did cooperate."

He sat on the sofa, arranged himself in a lazy sprawl. "If this is about Tiara Kent, I have witnesses putting me here in the club at the time she was killed. You spoke with one yourself just last night."

Studying the paper, Eve answered without looking up. "Your alibi was killed early this morning."

"Really?" He sipped negligently. "That's a great pity. She was an excellent bartender."

"Where were you between two and four A.M. this morning?"

"Here, of course. I have a business to run and patrons to entertain."

Now her eyes flashed to his. Let him see, she told herself. Let him see that I *know*. That I won't back down. "And witnesses to intimidate?"

"As you like." He shrugged a shoulder, and there was a laugh on his face now, a gleeful amusement smeared with viciousness. "I find religious prejudice tedious, but understandably . . . human. Those outside the cult often fear it, or smirk at it. For myself, I enjoy it and find it profitable. And there are other, more intimate benefits."

He rose again, moved across the room, opened a door. "Kendra, would you come out for a moment?"

She was covered in a robe so thin it might've been air, and it showed a generously curved body. Her hair was tumbled, her eyes blurry with sleep, and — Eve was certain — chemicals.

She recognized the blonde that had approached and pawed over Dorian the night before. She moved to him now, wrapped her arms around his neck, rubbed her body suggestively to his. "Come back to bed."

"Soon. This is Lieutenant Dallas, and her associates. Kendra Lake, a friend of mine. Kendra, the lieutenant would like to know where I was this morning, between two and four."

She turned her head, aimed eyes with pupils big enough to swim in toward Eve. "Dorian was with me, in bed, having sex. Lots of sex. We'd be having sex now if you'd go away. Unless you want to stay and watch."

"What are you on, Kendra?" Eve asked.

"I don't need to be on anything but Dorian." She rose on her toes, whispered something in Dorian's ear. He laughed, a low rumble, then shook his head.

"That's rude. Why don't you go back in, wait for me. I won't be long."

"Kendra," Eve said as the blonde started back toward the bedroom. "Did he promise you'd live forever?"

Kendra looked over her shoulder, smiled. Then shut the bedroom door behind her.

"Was there something else, Lieutenant?" Dorian asked. "I hate to keep a beautiful woman waiting."

"This might hold up." She set the document down. "Or it may not. Either way, we're not done. You shouldn't have used Gregor Pensky's DNA, because I'm going to link you to him." She stepped closer, ignoring the tickle at the back of her throat as those dark eyes pierced hers. "We'll talk again real soon, Dorian."

He grabbed her hand, brought it to his lips. She told herself she hadn't yanked it away to prove a point. But she wasn't entirely sure.

"I'll look forward to it."

Watching him, she dipped a finger in his cup, sucked the liquid off her finger. "Tasty," she said as his eyes blurred with what she recognized as excitement.

She walked out, down the stairs. With an effort she kept her expression cool as he once again materialized in front of her, in the mists that now clouded the club.

"I always escort my guests to the door. Safe travels, Lieutenant. Until we meet again."

"How'd he do that?" Even as her eyes tracked the tunnels, Peabody stuttered out the question. "How'd he do that?"

"Elevator, false doors. Smoke and fucking mirrors." It irritated Eve that he'd nearly made her jump, disturbed her so that her skin crawled as if he'd run his fingers over it.

She had to remind herself she'd bearded him in his own den, and she hadn't cracked. Her pulse wasn't steady, but she hadn't cracked.

"Damn good trick though," Baxter commented from the rear. "Did you get a load of the blonde? I might try a little blood sucking if you score that kind of action."

"She's an idiot, and a lucky one," Eve tossed back. "He needs to keep her alive, unless he's bone stupid."

"She was using. You were right on that one, Lieutenant." Trueheart's voice was just a little breathy. "I saw plenty of zoners and chemi-heads when I did sidewalk sleeper detail. She was zoned to the eyeballs."

"Okay, so he likes his women toked, and plays magic tricks. Not so scary," Peabody decided. "And the stuff he was drinking? Syrup, right? Just red syrup."

"No." Eve avoided a smear of some unidentifiable substance on the tunnel floor and aimed for the dim light ahead. "That was blood."

"Oh." Peabody gripped the cross at her neck. "Well."

On the street, Eve snapped out orders as she moved to her vehicle. "Baxter, I want you and Trueheart to find me a connection, any connection between Vadim and Pensky. Use EDD, if necessary, and see if you can pin Vadim in the area Pensky was killed. I'll get you the data I have. Peabody, push harder on the jewelry from the first vic. Turning the glitters liquid may be too hard to resist. We need to run this Kendra moron. My money says she's got a deep well. His pattern is to bilk rich women. However he's escalated, whatever the game, that's his base."

She shoved her way into traffic. "I'm going to the PA. I need a damn warrant, and I want to shatter his religious shield into a lot of tiny pieces."

But an hour later, Eve stood, stunned and furious, in APA Cher Reo's office.

"You've got to be kidding me."

"I'm giving it to you straight." Reo was smart, savvy, and ambitious, a small blonde dynamo. And she tossed up her hands. "I'm not saying we couldn't have the order overturned, I'm saying it's a tricky business, and one that would take time and a lot of taxpayer dollars. The boss won't move on it, not with what you have. Bring us evidence, even a real glimmer of probable cause on the homicides, and we'll start the war. And war is the word. The courts don't like to mess with religious objections and predilections, even when they're obvious bullshit."

"This guy bled two women to death."

"Maybe he did. You say he did, I'm going to agree with you. But I can't give you a warrant for his residence, his place of business, on what you've got. I can't break down his objection to daylight hours with what you've got. Worse, the DNA you took — the vial with your initials on it, doesn't match."

"He switched them."

"How?"

"I don't know how." She kicked Reo's desk.

"Hey!"

"Reo, this guy's just getting started. He's pumped. He's using God knows what to keep pumped, and the killing's got him flying on his own importance. He's got a club full of opportunities every damn night. Like a damn all-you-can-eat buffet."

"Bring me something. I'll go to the wall for you, you know that. Bring me something I can use. Until you do, I'll do some research on precedents for breaking through a religious objection. If you can wiggle something

223

that rings on the use or possession of illegals, I'll get you a warrant to search and seize on those grounds. It's the best I can do, Dallas."

"Okay. Okay." Eve raked her hands through her hair. "I'll get something." She thought of Allesseria's ex. Illegals passed around like party favors, he'd said. Add three cops and another civilian who had been in the club and they'd all swear they'd witnessed illegals bought, sold, and consumed. "Yeah, I can get something for an illegals raid."

"Make it work. And you know," Reo cast a glance at her office window, "I think I'm going to be damn sure I'm home and behind a locked door before sunset."

# CHAPTER
# NINE

Eve hunted up Feeney and Roarke in a lab in EDD. She could see them both standing, hands in pockets, as they studied a screen — in the same way she'd noted men often studied motors or other gadgets.

Physically, they couldn't have been less alike with Feeney nearly a head shorter even with the explosion of the mixed ginger and silver bush of his hair. Feeney habitually slouched, just as he was habitually rumpled and wrinkled. Roarke may have ditched his suit jacket and rolled up the sleeves of his crisp white shirt, but the contrast remained very broad.

Inside, she knew they often ran on the same path, particularly when it came to e-work. Geeks born of the same motherboard, she thought.

It was a relief to see them, and not so hard to admit. A relief to see these two men — so essential to the life she'd made — after coming from her confrontation with Dorian, and the demons he woke in her.

She stepped in. "Did you clean up the transmission?"

Feeney turned to her, droopy eyes, mournful expression. Roarke shifted, eyes of an almost savage blue. There was a click here, too, but a good solid one, one that made her smile.

Roarke angled his head. "Lieutenant?"

"Nothing." But she thought: *Who needs crosses and holy water to fight demons when you have two men like this?* Dorian would never have understood that bright and brilliant human link. Her father had never understood it.

"So." She crossed to them, and because it amused her, slid her hands into her pockets to mirror their stances. "What's the word?"

"Good news," Feeney began. "We got her clean. Bad news, there's not much of him."

"I don't need much."

"Going to need more than what we've got. Computer, run enhanced transmission."

Acknowledged . . .

Eve watched Allesseria's face. It was crystal clear now, as was the night around her, as was her voice. A streetlight beamed over her. The movement — rather than the jerky bounce of her quick walk — had been smoothed out, slowed down.

There was a sound, a whoosh of air, a ripple of fabric on the breeze. Eve watched the gloved hand snake in, between the 'link and the victim's face. There was an upward jerk, an instant of pain and terror in Allesseria's eyes. Then the image flipped as the phone tumbled: sky, street, sidewalk. Black.

"Crap" was Eve's comment, and her hands fisted in her pockets now. "Anything when you magnify and slow it down?"

226

"We can enhance so you can count the stitches in the seams of the glove," Feeney told her. "Can use the scale program to get you the size of it. We can give you the attacker's probable height calculated from the size, the angles. But we can't put on screen what's not there. Got some snatches of audio though, for what it's worth."

He set the comp again, made the adjustments, then played it back.

What she heard first was silence.

"We backed out her voice, her footsteps," Roarke explained, "the ambient city noises. Now . . ."

She caught it. Feet on pavement, the faintest rustle, then the rush she identified as a run followed by a jump or leap. There was a breath, expelled in a kind of laugh as the hand shot out and clamped Allesseria's throat. And as the images rolled and tumbled on screen, a single low word. *You.*

"Not enough for a voiceprint," Feeney pointed out. "Never hold up in court even if we could match it on one syllable."

"He doesn't have to know that." Eve narrowed her eyes at the screen. "Maybe what we've got is just enough to shake him, to make him think we have more."

Feeney grinned at Roarke, tapped a finger to his temple. "She's got something cooking up there."

"Yeah, I do. This time, we con the con."

Roarke stepped into Eve's office, closed the door. "I don't like it."

She continued across the cramped little room to her AutoChef, programmed coffee. "It's a good plan. It'll work." She took the two mugs of hot black out, passed him one. "And I didn't figure you'd like it. That's one of the drawbacks of having you inside an investigation."

"There are other ways to run him to ground, Eve."

"This is the quickest. There's no putting standard surveillance on him," she began. "There are dozens of ways in and out of those tunnels. I can't know what kind of escape hatch he might have in that club, up in his apartment. He decides he's bored here, or there's too much heat, he'd be in the wind before we got close."

"Find a way to shut down the club. Illegals raid will put him out of business."

"Sure, we could do that, we *will* do that. And if that's all we do, he'll be smoke. There are fronts to the business," she pointed out. "You said so yourself. And it'd take time we don't have to cut through them and dig down to him. By then he's gone."

He set the coffee down on her desk. "All right, even agreeing that all that's true, or very likely, it doesn't justify you going in alone. You're setting it up this way because the DNA crashed on you, and you're blaming yourself."

"That's not true." Or not entirely, she amended silently. "Sure, it pisses me off he pulled that over on me, but I'm not doing this to even the score." Or not entirely.

Logic, she decided, was the best way to lay it out. Not as satisfying as a fight, she thought, but quicker. "Okay, look. I go in there with troops or other badges, he's not going to talk, even if he sticks around long enough for me to corner him. He doesn't have to stick around at this point. I can't even pry him aboveground and get him in the box for interview. It has to be on his turf, and it has to be between him and me."

"Why — on the last point?"

"Why didn't you like him, from the get?"

She could see irritation cross Roarke's face before he picked up the coffee again. "Because he scoped my wife."

"Yeah. He'd like to take a bite, not only because I'm the cop looking at him, but because I'm married to you. Be a big ego kick for him to score off you. And if he thinks he has a shot at that, he'll take it, and I'll be ready."

"Eve —"

"Roarke. He'll kill again and soon. Maybe tonight. He has a taste for it now. You saw that, and so did I, the first time we met him. I'm telling you I saw more of it today. I see what he is."

This was the core, he knew, whatever she said. Whatever the other truths, this was the heart of it for her. "He's not your father."

"No, but there's a breed, and they're both of it. The smoke, the blood, the insinuation: Is he or isn't he an undead, bloodsucking fiend? That may tingle the spine, rouse superstitions, even tease the logical to entertain the illogical. But it's what's under it, Roarke. It's, well, shit, it's the beast that lives there that has to be stopped."

"The one you have to face," he corrected. "How many times?"

"As many as it takes. I want to walk away from it. Hell, I get within five feet of him, I want to run from it. And because I do, I can't."

"No." He traced his thumb down the shallow dent in her chin. "You can't." That, he knew, was what he had to face — again and again. Loving her left him no choice. "But this rush —"

"He's flying on the moment. Whatever drugs he's on, they're not as potent as the kill. As the blood. If I don't try this, and he gets another, how do I live with that?"

He searched her face, then lifted a hand to her cheek. "Being you, you don't. You can't. But I still don't have to like it."

"Understood. And . . ." She took his hand, squeezed it briefly. "Appreciated. Let's just count on me doing my job, and the rest of you doing yours. We'll shut him down, nail down that lid, before he knows what the hell's going on."

"He best not get so much as a nibble of you. That's my job." He leaned down, caught her bottom lip between his teeth. After one quick nip, he sank in, drawing her close, taking them both deep.

Her initial amusement slid away into the dreamy until she could float away on the taste of him, glide off on the promise. When she sighed, eased back, her lips curved up.

"Good job," she told him.

230

"I do my best."

"Maybe later you can put in some overtime."

"Being dedicated to my work, I'll be available."

"But for right now, let's go get the team together for a full briefing. I don't want any screwups."

"Lieutenant." He caught her hand before she reached the door, and tugged her back around. Out of his pocket he drew a silver cross on a silver chain, and dangled it in front of her.

"Knew I forgot something." But when he draped it over her head, she goggled. "What? You're serious?"

"Indulge me." He planted another kiss on her lips, this one brief and firm. "I'm a superstitious man with a logical mind that can entertain the illogical."

Staring at him, she shook her head. "You're full of surprises, pal. Just full of them."

She used a conference room for the briefing. On screen was a diagram of Bloodbath, and a second of the apartment — or the area of the apartment Eve had seen. Both were sketched from memory, with input from the others on the team who'd been inside the club.

As was often the case with underground establishments, no recorded blueprints or work orders could be located.

"There will be alternate exits," Eve continued. "It's likely at least some of the staff are aware of them, and will use them. Detaining and arresting waitresses and naked dancers aren't priorities."

"Speak for yourself," Baxter shot out, "on the naked dancers angle."

"Moving civilians out," Eve said, ignoring him, "without inciting a riot is a primary goal. Anyone wants to make collars for illegals, that's a personal decision and can be determined at the time. A couple dozen busts will add weight to the op, and hang on Vadim as manager. Anything and everything we get on him is a plus, but not at the expense of the primary target."

She scanned faces. "Nobody moves in, nobody tips the scales until I give the go. My communicator will be open for said go. Nothing, I repeat, nothing, is to be recorded from that source. I'm not having this slime skate on a technicality."

She paused, ordered the computer to show the diagram of the club only. "Our warrant covers only this area. No personnel are to move outside the club area in search or pursuit without probable cause. All weapons low stun."

Once more, she switched the screen image. Now Dorian Vadim's face filled it. "This is primary target. Unless specifically ordered or cleared, he is not to be detained or apprehended. If I can't pull this off, we have no cause for arrest. Suit up," she ordered. "Vests all around. Report to squad leaders for transportation to target."

She laid a hand on her sidearm. "Let's go kick ass."

As she bent to check her clutch piece, Baxter tapped her shoulder.

"What?"

"Got something for you." He held it out as she straightened.

"You're a laugh a minute, Baxter."

"Yeah, you gotta admit." He gave the wooden stake an agile toss.

Because she was amused despite herself, she caught the stake in one hand, then stuck it in her belt. "Thanks."

He blinked, then roared with laughter. "Eve Dallas, Vampire Slayer. One for the books."

# CHAPTER
# TEN

She went in alone, the way it had to be, as a cop, as a woman fighting her own demons.

She walked the now-familiar path down from the world to the underground, through the fetid tunnels with misery skulking in dirty shadows.

She'd come out of the shadows, Eve thought. So she knew what hid there, what bred there. What thrived there.

Light killed shadows, and it created them. But what loved the dark would always scuttle back from the light. Her badge had given her the light, Eve knew. Then Roarke had simply, irreversibly, blasted that light straight through her.

Nothing could pull her back again, unless she allowed it. Not the nightmares, not the memories, not whatever smear the man who'd made her had left in her blood.

What she did now, for the job, for two women, for herself, was only another way to cast the light.

She moved toward the ugly pulse of red and blue, the bone-rattling thrum of violent music.

The same bouncers flanked the arched door, and this time they sneered.

"Alone this time?"

Still moving, she kicked the one on the left solidly in the groin, smashed her elbow up and out into the bridge of the second's nose.

"Yeah," she said as she strode through the path they made as they stumbled back. "Just little old me."

She walked through the jostling crowd, through the sting of smoke, the crawl of fog. Someone made the mistake of making a playful grab for her and got a boot down hard on his instep for his trouble. And she never broke stride.

She reached the steps, started up their tight curve.

She felt him first, like the dance of sharpened nails along the skin. Then he was there, standing at the top of the stairs, mists swirling dramatically around him.

"Lieutenant Dallas, you're becoming a regular. No escort tonight?"

"I don't need an escort." She stopped on the step below him, knowing it gave him the superior ground. "But I'd like some privacy."

"Of course. Come with me." He held out a hand.

She placed hers in it, fought off a jitter of revulsion as his fingers twined with hers. He led her back, away from the crowd, then keyed in a code on his private door. "Enter Dorian," he said for the voice command, and the locks gave.

Inside candles were lit, dozens of them. Light and shadow, Eve thought again. On the wall screen various sections of the club were displayed, the sound muted, so people danced, groped, screamed, stalked, in absolute silence.

"Some view." Casually, she stepped away from him and stepped over as if to study the action on screen.

"My way of being surrounded and alone at the same time." His hand brushed lightly over her shoulder as he walked behind her and over to his bar. "You'd understand that."

"You talk as if you know me. You look at me as though you do. But you don't."

"Oh, I think I do. I saw the understanding of violence, of power, and the taste for it in you. We have that in common. Wine?"

"No. Are you alone here, Dorian?"

"I am." Despite her answer, he poured two glasses. "Though I planned to entertain a woman later." This time his gaze traveled over her, boldly intimate. "How interesting it should be you. Tell me, Eve, is this a professional or a personal call?"

She let herself stare at him, into those eyes. "I don't know. I guess we'll find out. I know you killed those women."

He smiled slowly. "Do you? How?"

"I feel it. I see it when I look at you. Tell me how you did it."

"Why should I? Why would I? Lieutenant."

As if impatient, she shook her head. "I don't have a warrant. You know that. I haven't given you your rights. I can't use anything you tell me. You know that, too. I just need to know what you are. Why I feel the way I do around you. I don't believe in . . ."

There was no mistaking the *hunger* on his face as he walked toward her. "In what?"

She could hear her father's voice whispering in her mind. *There are things in the dark, little girl. Terrible things in the dark.*

"In the sort of thing you're selling out there." She gestured toward the screen. "Turn that off, will you? It feels crowded in here."

"You don't like to watch?" he said, silkily. "Or be watched?"

"Depends," she answered with what she hoped sounded like false bravado.

"Screen off," he ordered, and smiled again. "Better?"

"Yeah. It's better with it off."

"That's the signal." Feeney nodded to Roarke. "All units, move in. Move in. She's playing him," he said to Roarke. "She'll walk him right into it."

"Or he's playing her." With Eve's voice in his ear, Roarke rushed into the dark.

Into the terrible things.

"Hold it." There was the slightest hesitation in her order as she slapped a hand against Dorian's chest and shoved. "I have obligations. I have loyalties."

"None of which fill your needs."

"You don't know my needs."

"Give me five minutes to do as I like with you, and you'll know differently. You came to me." He trailed his fingers over her cheek. "You came to me alone. You want to know what I can give you."

237

She shook her head, stepped away. "I came because I need to understand. I can't settle, I can't focus. I feel like something's trying to crawl out of my skin."

"I can help you with that."

She glanced over her shoulder at him. "Yeah, I bet you could. But I'm not like Tiara Kent. I'm not looking for cheap thrills. And I'm not like Allesseria Carter. I don't need your goodwill. I'm not afraid of you."

"Aren't you? Aren't you afraid of what I could make you?"

She looked at the portrait. "Like that?" Her voice was just a little breathless. "I'm not that gullible."

He lifted one of the wineglasses, drank deeply. "There's more in the world that slips in and out of what's deemed reality."

"Such as?"

He drank again, and his eyes went even darker. "Such as powers, and hungers beyond the human. I'll take you there. I can show you a glimpse without causing you harm. You should drink. Relax. Nothing will happen to you here. It's not my way."

"No, you go to them. Kent practically spread rose petals on a path to her bed for you."

"Hypothetically, invitations are required."

"In an occupied building," Eve agreed. "Not in an abandoned one. Like the one where you dragged Allesseria, where you killed her."

"Does it excite you to think so, to look at me and see her death?"

"Maybe it does."

238

"You seek death." He laid his fingertips under hers, lifted her hand. "Surround yourself with it. Isn't that what I sensed, what I saw in you that first moment our eyes met? It connects us, this . . . fondness for death in a way the man you give yourself to can never understand. He can't reach that dark bloom inside you. I can."

She let her fingers curl to his for an instant, then eased back again. "I don't know what connects us, but I felt something when I heard your voice come in on Allesseria's 'link message to me. It was a mistake to say anything, Dorian, a mistake not to make certain the 'link was down and the transmission broken before you spoke to her. We'll have your voiceprint match by morning."

He lowered the glass he'd lifted to his lips. "That's not possible."

"Would I be here now otherwise? Risking all this so I could see you tonight? This goes down tomorrow, and my part in it's over. I need answers for me. Why would I tell you we have evidence building that could take you down, give you time to poof? I have to know. For me."

"I have an alibi," he insisted.

"Kendra Lake? Another spoiled rich girl running on hormones, vanity, and chemicals. She won't help you. She'll crack, we both know it. She's on the juice, she's your lover. It won't hold."

"You're lying." He gulped down the rest of the liquid in the glass, heaved the glass aside. "You're lying. You bitch."

Okay, Eve thought, time to change directions.

★ ★ ★

Outside the apartment it was hell. Screams and shouts echoed through the mist some clever soul had boosted up when the small army of cops had burst in, announcing a raid.

Roarke flung one attacker aside, dodged the swipe of a knife from another. Preferring fists to stunner, he used them viciously. Despite the cacophony, he heard Eve's voice clearly in his head.

"She's losing him," he yelled to Feeney. Whirling, Roarke sprinted for the stairs through streams of stunner fire.

"Caught me," Eve said. "I'm lying about any pretense I find you attractive or compelling on a personal level. About the rest, that's a wrap. You not only ran your mouth where it could be heard on Allesseria's 'link, EDD's working on cleaning and enhancing a few seconds on screen during the trans. You moved partially into view.

"Added to that," she continued, "we're about to link you to one Pensky, Gregor. Shouldn't have used a former known associate as a fall guy. Even a dead fall guy, Dorian. Little slips, they'll kill you every time."

She glanced idly around the room. "I bet you saved some of Tiara Kent's blood for a souvenir. I get that warrant in the morning, I'm going to find it, and the jewelry you took off her dead or dying body. You scum. That'll put you down for three counts of murder. Anything else you want to add to the menu?"

"Do you think you can threaten me?" His eyes were black pools. "Play with me?"

"If you're trying for thrall, you're missing. I'll have you locked on Allesseria in a matter of hours. The rest will tumble right into the pile. You're done. I just wanted the satisfaction of telling you personally before — Don't," she warned. She laid her hand on her stunner when she saw the move in his eyes. "Unless you want to add assaulting an officer to the mix. In which case, I can haul you out of here. Sun's down, Dorian."

"Yes, it is." He smiled, and to Eve's absolute shock, showed fangs.

He leaped, almost seemed to fly at her. She drew her weapon, pivoted, but she wasn't quick enough. Nothing could have been. She got off two shots as he hurled her across the room. He took both hits, and just kept coming. She felt it in every bone as she hit the stone wall, and though the stunner spurted out of her hand on impact, she managed to roll, then kick up hard with both feet. The force knocked him back far enough to give her room to flip up.

She braced for the next attack, but instead he hissed like a snake, cringed back. She flicked her gaze down, saw he was staring at the cross that had come out from under her shirt.

"You've got to be kidding me." He snarled as he circled her. "You actually believe your own hype."

Whatever he'd drunk had juiced him up good, she determined. So good, she'd never be able to take him in hand-to-hand. She held up the cross as she tried to gauge the distance to her stunner, and her chances of reaching it.

241

"I'll drink you dry." His tongue ran over his long incisors. "Almost dry. And make you drink me. I'll change you into what I am."

"What? A babbling lunatic? Why didn't Tiara change?"

"She wasn't strong enough. I drank too much of her. But she died in bliss under me. As you will. But you're strong, strong enough to be reborn. I knew it when I saw you. Knew you'd be the first who'd walk as I walk."

"Uh-huh. You have the right to remain silent."

He sprang, leaping like a great cat. She blocked the first blow, though she felt the force of it sing down her arm, explode into her shoulder. But the second sent her sprawling. She thudded hard against one of his metal tables, and tasted her own blood in her mouth as she rolled painfully onto her back.

He was standing over her now, fangs gleaming, eyes mad. "I give you the gift, the ultimate kiss."

Eve swiped the blood off her mouth. "Bite me."

Grinning, he fell on her.

Outside the door, Feeney pulled out his master and a bag of electronic tricks to bypass the locks.

"I've got it." Blood seeped through the ragged tear in Roarke's jacket where a knife point had slipped through. He flipped out a recorder, closed his eyes to focus first on the tones of the beeps.

Quickly, he played his fingers over the keypad in the same order, then held the recorder to the voice command.

"Enter Dorian," the recorder replayed.

"Hey, Dallas said nothing was to be recorded."

Roarke spared one glance over at Feeney's wide grin. "I'm a poor team player."

They pushed in the door, Roarke going low as he knew Feeney preferred high.

She was flat on her back, blood soaking her shirt. Even as Roarke rushed toward her, she pushed herself up on her elbows. "I'm okay. I'm okay. Call the MTs before that asshole bleeds to death."

Roarke barely spared a glance at the man lying on the floor with a wooden stake in his belly. His own stomach muscles were knotted in slippery fists. "How much of this is yours?"

She looked down at her shirt in some disgust. "Hardly any. Missed the heart. Bastard was on top of me. Gut wounds are messy. Feeney?"

"Contacting the MTs," he told her. "Situation below is nearly contained. Hell of a show. But looks like you're the headliner here. Jesus, what a freaking mess."

"I can't believe I'm going to have to thank Baxter for being a smart-ass. Lost my weapon. He'd've done some damage before you got through if I hadn't had the pointy stick."

She started to stand, and with Roarke's help made it to her feet. Once there, she swayed and she staggered. "Just a little shaken up. Hit my head on various hard objects. No, no, don't carry me."

He simply scooped her into his arms. "You're doomed to have me disobey." Then he pressed his lips to the side of her throat where he saw the faint wounds. "Got a taste of you, did he?"

She heard the rage, and tried to tamp it down. "Told him to bite me. It's the first time anyone's ever taken that suggestion literally. Except you." She turned Roarke's face with her hand so that he looked at her rather than Dorian. "Put me down, will you, pal? This seriously undermines my authority."

"Hey, hey!" Crouched over Dorian, Feeney stopped even his half-hearted attempt to stanch the blood flow. "Is this guy sporting fangs?"

"He must've had them filed down that way," Eve said. "Then had them capped. Easy on, easy off. We'll sort it out."

Peabody ran in. There was a darkening bruise on her cheekbone and a nasty scrape along her jaw. "Unit's heading out to escort the MTs in. Holy crap!" she added when she saw Dorian. "You staked him. You actually staked him."

"It was handy. Let's get those medics in here. I don't want this guy skipping out on multiple murder charges by dying on me. I want to know the minute he's able to talk. I think we're going to get an interesting confession."

"It's supposed to be the heart," she heard Peabody mutter. "It's really supposed to be the heart."

Eve blew out a long breath. "Keep it up, Peabody, and I may have Mira shrink your head after she's done with this second-rate Dracula. I want some damn air. I'm going up to the real world."

Once she had, she took the bottle of water Roarke passed her and drank like a camel. She lifted her chin at the blood on his sleeve. "Is that bad?"

"It damn well is. I liked this jacket. Here, take a blocker. If you don't have the mother of all headaches yet, it's only due to adrenaline. Take the blocker, and I won't haul your stubborn ass into a health center for an exam."

She popped the blocker without a quibble. Then since it was there, she sat on the edge of the floor through the open door of the police van.

"He believed it," she said after a moment. "He actually believed he was a vampire. Drugs probably pushed the act into his reality. Mira nailed the profile from the get. It was the pretending to be the Prince of Darkness that was the pretense, for him."

"More likely he was just pushing the con as far as it would take him — and gambling to use it to plead insanity."

"No. You didn't see his face when he looked at this." She held up the cross. "And thanks, by the way. It bought me a few minutes when it counted."

Roarke sat beside her, rubbed a hand over her thigh. "Illogical superstition. Sometimes it works."

"Apparently. He's got himself some kind of super-Zeus recipe, is my guess. Not just the whacked brain it causes, or the temporary strength. Speed, too. The bastard was fast. Magician training, grift experience, drugs. I wonder when it turned on him, stopped being a way to case marks."

Gently, Roarke traced a fingertip over her neck wounds. "There are all kinds of vampires, aren't there? Darling Eve."

"Yeah." Very briefly, since all of the cops running around were too busy to notice, she leaned her head against Roarke's shoulder. "Under it, he wasn't really like my father. Not the way I thought. My father wasn't crazy. Dorian, he's bug-shit."

"Evil doesn't have to be sane."

"No, you're right about that." And she'd faced it — and she'd beaten it. One more time. "Well, the bad news is he's going to end up in a facility for violent mental defectives, not a concrete cage. But you take what you can get."

Roarke's hand rested on her knee. She laid hers over it, squeezed. "And right now, I'll take a hot shower and a fresh shirt. I've got to go in and clean myself up, and clean this up, too."

"I'll drive."

"You should go home," she told him, but her hand stayed over his. "Get some sleep. It's going to take hours to close this up."

"I have this image I can't shake." He got up, drew her to her feet. "Of the sun rising, all red and gold smears over the sky. And you and I walking toward home in that lovely soft light. So taking what I can get, I'll take sunrise with you."

"Sunrise it is."

She kept her hand in his as she pulled out her communicator to contact Feeney, Peabody and the team leaders to check on the status below.

With her hand linked with Roarke's, the demons that plagued her were silent. And would stay silent, she thought, through the night. And well past sunrise.

# FESTIVE IN DEATH

## J. D. Robb

It's Christmas, but Lieutenant Eve Dallas is in no mood to celebrate. While her charismatic husband Roarke plans a huge, glittering party, Eve has murder on her mind. The victim — personal trainer Trey Ziegler — was trouble in life and is causing even more problems in death. Vain, unfaithful and vindictive, Trey had cultivated a lot of enemies. Which means Eve has a lot of potential suspects. And when she and Detective Peabody uncover Trey's sinister secret, the case takes a deadly turn. Christmas may be a festival of light, but Eve and Roarke will be forced once more down a very dark path in their hunt for the truth.

# CONCEALED IN DEATH

## J. D. Robb

There is nothing unusual about billionaire Roarke supervising work on his new property — but when he takes a ceremonial swing at the first wall to be knocked down, he uncovers the body of a girl. And then another — in fact, twelve dead girls concealed behind a false wall.

Luckily for Roarke, he is married to the best police lieutenant in town. Eve Dallas is determined to find the killer — especially when she discovers that the building used to be a sanctuary for delinquent teenagers and the parallel with her past as a young runaway hits hard.

As the girls' identities are slowly unravelled by the department's crack forensic team, Eve and her staunch sidekick Peabody get closer to the shocking truth.

# RITUAL IN DEATH AND MISSING IN DEATH

## J. D. Robb

A duo of two superb short stories featuring celebrated lieutenant, Eve Dallas

*Ritual in Death*: When a naked, knife-wielding man who thinks he has killed someone crashes a glamorous ball she's attending, Lieutenant Eve Dallas is almost relieved. The clues point towards ritual murder, but Eve knows there is nothing supernatural about a deadly lust for power . . .

*Missing in Death*: Aboard the Staten Island ferry, a tourist sees something she shouldn't have — and soon no one can find her. But if she didn't jump, and she's not on board, where is she? Lieutenant Eve Dallas and her team know that all the answers lie in just what was seen on that ferry . . .

# THANKLESS IN DEATH

## J. D. Robb

*Murder doesn't stop for Thanksgiving.*

As the household of NYPSD Lieutenant Eve Dallas and her billionaire husband Roarke prepares for an invasion of family and friends, an ungrateful son decides to stop the nagging from his parents — by ending their lives. Soon Jerald Reinhold is working his way through anyone who has ever thwarted him in his path to an easy life. Eve is increasingly frustrated in her efforts to cover all the potential victims as Jerald stays a terrifying step ahead. As the festivities begin, Eve is desperate to identify which victim will be next on Jerald's long list, so she can stop the killing spree . . .

# CALCULATED IN DEATH

## J. D. Robb

On a bitterly cold night on the steps outside an empty office in New York's financial district, a woman lies dead. It seems like a mugging gone wrong, but Eve Dallas soon discovers that the body was dumped at the newly renovated property. Now she has to find out why. Eve has a host of suspects for the murder. Using her husband Roarke's business know-how, and with colleague and friend Detective Delia Peabody by her side, Eve starts examining the motives of some very powerful people in order to catch a killer.

# DELUSION IN DEATH

## J. D. Robb

The scene that greets Lieutenant Eve Dallas one terrible evening in New York is more shocking than anything she has ever witnessed. The downtown bar is strewn with bodies — office workers have been sliced, bludgeoned or hacked to death, turning on each other in a desperate blinding rage. As Eve and her husband Roarke — who owns the bar — investigate the city, they link the attacks back to the Urban Wars and the chemical warfare used all those years ago. With another slaughter imminent, Eve must turn to unexpected sources to stop a killer pursuing revenge by creating mass carnage . . .